BIGGLES – FLYING DETECTIVE

There was a blinding flash. With it came a thundering explosion. A blast of air hit the Mosquito and lifted it clean off the ground. For perhaps three seconds it hung in the atmosphere, at an angle to its original course, wallowing sickeningly. Then it settled down, struck the ground with one wheel, bounced, swerved, and came to rest with its tail cocked high.

Dazed, his ears ringing, in something like a panic Ginger pushed himself back from the instrument panel against which he had been flung, and tried to get out. The door had jammed. Biggles's voice cut in, it seemed from a distance.

'Sit tight,' he ordered.

Ginger looked at him and saw that he was removing a splinter of glass from his cheek. There was blood on his face. He looked shaken.

'What happened?' gasped Ginger.

'Nothing – only that we've landed in a mine-field,' returned Biggles.

BIGGLES BOOKS PUBLISHED IN THIS EDITION:

Biggles: The Camels are Coming ✓
Biggles in France
Biggles Learns to Fly ✓
Biggles and the Rescue Flight ✓✓
Biggles Flies East ✓
Biggles of the Fighter Squadron
Biggles: The Cruise of the Condor ✓✓
Biggles & Co. ✓✓
Biggles in Spain ✓
Biggles and the Secret Mission
Biggles Defies the Swastika ✓
Biggles Fails to Return .
Biggles Delivers the Goods ✓
Biggles Defends the Desert ✓
Biggles in the Orient
Biggles – Flying Detective ✓✓
Biggles: Spitfire Parade (a graphic novel)

Biggles adventures available on cassette from
Tellastory, featuring Tim Pigott-Smith as Biggles:

Biggles Learns to Fly
Biggles Flies East
Biggles Defies the Swastika
Biggles in Spain
Biggles – Flying Detective
Biggles and the Secret Mission

BIGGLES – FLYING DETECTIVE

CAPTAIN W. E. JOHNS

RED FOX

Red Fox would like to express their grateful thanks for help in preparing these editions to Jennifer Schofield, co-author of *Biggles: the life of Captain W. E. Johns*, published by Veloce Publications, Linda Shaughnessy of A. P. Watt Ltd and especially to John Trendler, editor of *Biggles & Co*, the quarterly magazine for Biggles enthusiasts.

A Red Fox Book

Published by Random House Children's Books
20 Vauxhall Bridge Road, London SW1V 2SA

A division of Random House UK Ltd
London Melbourne Sydney Auckland
Johannesburg and agencies throughout the world

© W. E. Johns 1947

First published by Hodder & Stoughton 1947
Red Fox edition 1994

1 3 5 7 9 10 8 6 4 2

Set in Baskerville Roman by Intype, London
Printed and bound in Great Britain by
Cox & Wyman Ltd, Reading, Berkshire

RANDOM HOUSE UK Limited Reg. No. 954009

ISBN 0 09 939461 8

Contents

Chapter 1
Crime À La Mode*

The station headquarters of 'Biggles's Squadron,' R.A.F., wore an air of abandoned disorder, like a cinema when the last of the audience has gone and only the staff remain. Cupboard doors gaped, revealing bare shelves; the blackout blind sagged at one end; ashes of the last fire littered the grate; books and papers, tied in bundles with string, made an untidy pile in a corner.

Squadron-Leader Bigglesworth, known throughout the R.A.F. as 'Biggles', tilted back in a chair with his legs on the desk from which the letter trays had been removed. Flying-Officer 'Ginger' Hebblethwaite had perched himself on a corner of it, one leg swinging idly. Flight-Lieutenant Algy Lacey sat in reverse on a hard chair, elbows on the back, chin in his hands. Flight-Lieutenant Lord Bertie Lissie leaned out of the open window regarding the forsaken landing-ground with bored disapproval. Biggles took out his cigarette-case, selected a cigarette, and tapped it on the back of his left hand with pensive attention.

'Well, chaps, I think that's all,' he remarked. 'The war's over. We can either proceed on indefinite leave while the Air Ministry is sorting things out, or we can ask for our demobilisation papers, go home, and forget

*French: fashionable crime.

all about it. I must admit that this feeling of anti-climax is hard to take. There doesn't seem to be any point in doing anything. I feel like a cheap alarm clock with a busted mainspring.'

'We shall have to do something,' observed Ginger moodily.

'You've said that before,' reminded Biggles, wearily.

'There will be civil flying,' put in Algy.

'The only excitement you're likely to get out of that is dodging the ten thousand other blokes who'll be doing the same thing,' sneered Biggles.

'They've shot all the bally foxes, so there won't be any huntin' for a bit,' sighed Bertie from the window. He leaned forward, gazing up the deserted road. 'I say, chaps, there's a jolly old car coming,' he observed. 'I can see a bloke in a bowler.'

'Some poor sap got off the main road and lost his way,' suggested Algy without enthusiasm.

'No, by jingo, you're wrong old boy—absolutely wrong,' declared Bertie. 'Strike me horizontal! If it isn't the Air Commodore Raymond himself, no less. Coming to see that we're leaving everything shipshape and what-not, I suppose.'

'If he's in civvies he must be out of the service already,' said Biggles, with a flicker of interest.

Air Commodore Raymond stopped the car, got out, and strode to the door of the squadron office. For a moment he stood on the threshold, smiling faintly as he regarded the officers in turn.

'What's this?' he inquired. 'An undertaker's parlour?'

Biggles took his feet off the desk and pulled up a

vacant chair. 'Take a pew, sir,' he invited. 'We're all washed up and browned off. Apart from an N.C.O.* and a small maintenance party, what you see is all that remains of the squadron. Nice of you to run down to say good-bye. We should have departed an hour ago had we been able to think of somewhere to go.'

'Haven't decided on anything yet, then?' murmured the Air Commodore as he sat down.

'We've got to do something,' interposed Ginger.

Biggles considered him with disfavour. 'If you say that again I'll knock your block off,' he promised.

'Well, what *are* you going to do?' inquired the Air Commodore.

'That,' returned Biggles slowly, 'is a question that should baffle the Brains Trust.**'

'Why?'

'Because there isn't any answer—at any rate, not at present. No doubt something will turn up, sooner or later.'

'I may have brought the answer,' suggested the Air Commodore softly.

Biggles's eyes narrowed. 'Are you kidding?'

'No,' answered the Air Commodore evenly. 'By the way, you may be interested to know that I'm back at my old job at Scotland Yard—Assistant Commissioner.'

'Congratulations,' offered Biggles. 'You didn't lose much time getting out of your war-paint.'

'There wasn't any time to lose,' was the terse reply.

---

*Non-Commissioned Officer e.g. a corporal or a sergeant.
**A BBC radio programme in which a panel of experts answered questions on any subject sent in by listeners.

'My chief was shouting for me, so the Air Ministry let me go right away.'

'Has this anything to do with your coming down here?'

'I didn't rush down to gaze at a row of empty hangars,' declared the Air Commodore. 'I've got a proposition.'

'We're listening,' asserted Biggles. 'Almost anything, bar directing the traffic in Trafalgar Square, will suit me.'

'Good. I've got a job I think you can handle. Suppose I run over the main features?'

'Go ahead, sir,' invited Biggles.

'When I went to the Yard last Monday to resume my duties, I soon discovered why the Commissioner was shouting for me,' began the Air Commodore. 'Before an hour was out I had taken over a case that is unique to the point of being startling. Naturally, even while the war was on I realised that as soon as it was over we should have flying crooks to contend with. With fifty thousand men—and women—of different nationalities able to fly aeroplanes, that was pretty obvious; but I confess I didn't expect a racket to start so soon; nor did I visualise anything on the scale that I shall presently narrate. In view of my air experience, the Commissioner hinted some time ago that he would ask me to undertake the formation of a flying squad— in the literal sense. The idea was to start with a few fully trained men and build up. We've some good officers at the Yard, but, of course, they're not experts in technical aviation. We shall have to start with youngsters and teach them aviation as well as police procedure. But that's by the way. My flying days are past, I'm afraid, so my position is really that of organiser.' The Air Commodore took one of Biggles's cigarettes.

'Obviously, the formation of such a force as we envisage will take time,' he continued. 'In the meanwhile, a smart crook, or a gang, is gathering a nice harvest with comparative impunity. The thing is urgent, and serious—so serious that I have slipped down to ask you if you would co-operate with me until we can get properly organised, equipped to deal with the new menace. You had better hear the story before you commit yourselves.'

'Let me get one point clear, sir,' interposed Biggles. 'Should we handle this job as officers of the R.A.F., or as civilians, or police—or what?'

'For pay and discipline you would come under the Yard, so it would mean leaving the Air Force. If you were willing I should enrol you in the Auxiliary Police, special service branch, attached to my department at the C.I.D. It would mean a drop in rank, *pro tem.** The best I could do for you would be detective-sergeant.'

Biggles smiled. 'That would be fun,' he murmured. 'Just think how my lads would laugh to see me sporting three stripes.'

'You wouldn't necessarily have to wear uniform,' the Air Commodore pointed out.

'Plain-clothes men, what-ho,' said Bertie softly.

'You've been reading thrillers,' accused the Air Commodore. 'You can call yourself what you like as far as I'm concerned if you'll nab these winged highwaymen. But really, this is no joking matter. If you're

*Latin: for the time being.

9

interested I'll run briefly over the facts.' The Air Commodore settled back in his chair.

'The thing started three weeks ago, before the ink on the peace papers was properly dry, so to speak,' he resumed. 'From that fact alone we may assume that the scheme was already cut and dried. It began in the Persian Gulf—of all places; and here we see at once how aircraft are going to enable crooks to extend their range of operations. As you probably know, Bigglesworth, once a year the big Indian jewel buyers go up to the Persian Gulf ports to bid for the pearl harvest. Between them they buy all the best stuff. Having done so they return by steamship to India, handing their parcels of pearls to the purser* for safe custody. The purser tags a number on each bag and puts it in his safe. Over many years this has become an established procedure, and up to the present there has never been any trouble. For that reason, precautions against theft may have got a bit slack. At any rate, such precautions as did exist were definitely obsolete. The run from Basra to India, in the *Rajah*, which is quite a small vessel, and very old—she has been doing the trip for years—takes ten days. When the *Rajah* docked at Bombay it was discovered that the back of the purser's safe—an old-fashioned affair not much better than a tin box—had been cut out. The pearls had gone—the entire year's catch, nearly half a million pounds' worth.'

Ginger whistled softly.

'Nice going, by Jove!' murmured Bertie.

---

*A naval officer responsible for managing money matters and keeping accounts.

'But surely no one could unload on the market such a quantity of pearls without the police hearing of it?' muttered Biggles. 'I mean, with such a parcel of pearls adrift the big dealers would be on the watch for them?'

'In the ordinary way, yes,' agreed the Air Commodore. 'But not in this case. Not only were the pearls—except the outstanding ones—disposed of before the theft was discovered, but a check-up reveals the almost incredible fact that the pearls, without going through customs, were offered for sale in the United States a week before the *Rajah* docked. In other words, the pearls were in America within three days of the *Rajah* leaving Basra. The thieves had a clear week in front of them to dispose of the swag before the robbery was discovered.'

'By gosh! That *was* quick work,' remarked Algy.

'You can imagine what a shock the Bombay police had when the facts were ascertained,' went on the Air Commodore. 'They were still searching the ship for the missing pearls, detaining the passengers, when it was learned that the gems had already been sold in America. The *Rajah* hadn't touched anywhere, so the thief must have dropped overboard at a pre-arranged rendezvous, where presumably he was picked up by an accomplice, either in a boat or a marine aircraft. Obviously, an aircraft comes into the picture eventually, because the only way the pearls could have got to the States in the time was by air—and not by a regular air-liner. There was no public service running from the Middle East to Europe, and on to the States, in that time. Anyway, no commercial aircraft could have covered the distance so quickly. Moreover, all air-

11

liners have to go through customs. It must have been a private plane—and no ordinary plane at that.'

'You're right there,' agreed Biggles, who was scribbling figures on a pad.

'It was the slickest job ever pulled off,' declared the Air Commodore. 'We rather felt that after such a nice haul the master-mind behind the robbery would lie low for a bit. But we were wrong—unless two crooks have had the same sort of brainwave. A week later, the South African Government plane that flies the diamonds— uncut stones—from Alexander Bay to Capetown, failed to show up. This also is a regular run, made only once or twice a year. The plane carries an armed guard and is escorted by a fighter. A search was made. The missing machines were found, crashed, within a few miles of each other. Judging by the line of flight the escort must have been disposed of first—riddled from behind. The pilot was shot through the back. It seems unlikely that he even saw his attacker. It had become a routine job and he may have been caught off his guard. The pilot and guards of the transport plane were also dead. The diamonds, three hundred and thirty thousand pounds' worth, had vanished. We have no evidence that the job was done by the same gang that looted the pearls, but a similarity of methods suggest that it might have been. Here again the stones were sold before the loss was discovered. The South African Air Force was fifty hours finding the crashes. The diamonds had just been disposed of in Buenos Aires and Rio de Janeiro. An interesting point is that, as in the case of the pearls, the best gems were retained. Maybe the gangsters decided they would attract too much attention if they were sold in the open market.'

'Suffering skylarks! Their plane must be something exceptional, both in speed and range!' exclaimed Biggles.

The Air Commodore nodded. 'You will begin to see what we're up against,' he said grimly. 'Here we have a crook who can transport himself, and his swag, to the other side of the world in a few hours. He could do a job in London tonight, and by dawn be six thousand miles away—in any direction. The police are on a spot. It looks as if we shall have to establish a network of radio-location* observation posts all round the Empire to watch for this mystery plane. That will cost a tidy penny.'

While the Air Commodore had been speaking the telephone had rung. Biggles picked up the receiver, listened, and passed it to the senior officer. 'For you, sir,' he said.

'I told the Yard they'd find me here if I was wanted,' remarked the Air Commodore. Then, in the phone, 'Hello—yes, Raymond here,' he listened for two or three minutes. 'All right, thanks,' he said quietly, and hung up. Turning to Biggles, he went on: 'That was the Yard. Yesterday, the pilot who flies the pay-roll from Nairobi, in Kenya, to the Jaggersfontein Copper Mines, in Northern Rhodesia, was shot down and killed. The plane was burnt out. He carried forty-three thousand pounds, most of it in silver, to pay the workmen. The silver may have melted in the heat—but it's gone.'

'Holy Icarus! This chap is certainly hot stuff,'

---

*Known today as RADAR, radio location is a method of detecting the range, height, speed and direction of an aeroplane by using radio waves.

averred Biggles. 'But just a minute! To pick up the silver—and the diamonds, for that matter—the outlaw plane must have landed. That must have been a nasty risk, in wild country.'

'In each case,' answered the Air Commodore bitterly, 'the shooting occurred over open country, terrain on which an emergency landing would be possible. That wasn't luck. This bandit knows his job. He chooses his spots.' The Air Commodore stubbed his cigarette viciously.

'One thing puzzles me,' murmured Biggles. 'You can't operate a high-performance aircraft without a base, and you can't run a motor without oil and petrol. Where's this chap getting his fuel and lubricant? He must have used a devil of a lot already. Only the big operating companies, apart from the Air Force, carry supplies on that scale. What have the airports to say about this? Haven't they seen the plane?'

'We've checked up,' asserted the Air Commodore. 'None of them has seen a strange plane. The queer thing is, oil and petrol are still under the control of the Allied Nations.* A certificate is needed to buy a large quantity. None has been released to an unauthorised person. Certainly none has been sold.'

'Hm. This gets curiouser and curiouser,' murmured Biggles. 'Obviously, the chap is getting juice somewhere. If we could locate the spot we should be on his track.'

'How are we going to locate it?' inquired the Air Commodore, a trifle sarcastically. 'It might be any-

---

*Referring to the victorious nations of World War II known as the Allies, notably Britain, USA and Russia who between them owned and controlled most of the world's output of oil during this period.

where between the North Pole and the South Sea Islands.'

'It certainly isn't easy to know where to start looking,' agreed Biggles.

'Personally, I haven't an idea,' confessed the Air Commodore.

Biggles raised his eyebrows. 'So you ask me? What do you think I can do about it? I'm no magician.'

'You're a technical expert on aviation as well as a pilot, and only a man with those qualifications has any hope of catching up with this bandit on wings,' declared the Air Commodore. 'Moreover, when you set about a thing seriously you have a knack of getting to the gristle, sooner or later. With all your experience, if anyone can do the job, it's you. As an inducement I can tell you that the insurance companies, who are getting worried, are offering a reward of ten thousand pounds for information leading to the conviction of this crook, plus ten per cent of the value of any gems or money recovered.'

'Should we be eligible for that—as official policemen?' asked Biggles shrewdly.

'I'll put it in your contract if you like.'

Biggles's face broke into a smile. 'That does make a difference,' he admitted. Turning to the others, 'How do you feel about it?'

'Top hole—absolutely top hole,' assented Bertie warmly.

'I don't think you need consult Algy and Ginger,' the Air Commodore told Biggles. 'Where you go they'll go. It's up to you.'

'All right, sir, I'll have a shot at it,' decided Biggles. 'Our enlistment into the police force will only be temporary, of course. There's a question I'd like to ask—an obvious one. I assume no one has seen this mystery plane, otherwise you'd have mentioned it?'

'We've made inquiries, but so far we've had only one report—and that isn't very promising. Of course, several people must have seen the machine, unless it was flying at a tremendous height; but how could we contact them? With so many aircraft in the sky the average man barely troubles to glance up when one goes over. The report I spoke about reached us in a curious way. On a ship, a collier, outward bound from Cardiff to Montevideo, there happened to be a man who *was* interested in aircraft. He was the first officer. During the war he served in the R.N.V.R.* as a plane spotter. On the day following the shooting down of the diamond plane—which, of course, this chap knew nothing about—he was on deck when the sound of an aircraft made him look up . . . sort of semi-professional interest, I suppose. He was just in time to see a plane, travelling at high speed, pass across a break in the clouds. He could not identify it, and this so worried him that to satisfy his curiosity he radioed the Air Ministry asking them to identify the aircraft. From his description the design must have been very unorthodox—so unusual that the Air Ministry couldn't identify it either. According to this man's description the machine had no fuselage. It was a twin-engined job, the two power eggs** projecting far in front of the nacelle.*** This nacelle was tapered down aft to a

*Royal Naval Volunteer Reserve.
**Slang: engines.
***The cockpit section.

single boom which carried the tail unit. The fin was exceptionally long, and narrow. It began half-way down the boom, and ended in a balanced rudder that was almost a perfect oval. That's all. It might have been the mystery plane, or an experimental job that we know nothing about.'

'Queer arrangement,' murmured Biggles. 'I'll bear it in mind. By the way, what are we going to do for aircraft?'

'The Air Force has more machines than it needs at the moment, so you can help yourself. I've already fixed that up with the Air Minister. He will provide us with documents that will enable you to refuel at any R.A.F. station, and call on service personnel for maintenance. That's a temporary arrangement. The police will need an air force of their own. I'm busy on that now. For the moment we have been allocated a hangar at Croydon, so you'd better regard that as your base. I don't suppose I shall see much of you, but officially, your headquarters will be at the Yard, so I'll fix you up with an office.'

Ginger grinned. 'Imagine me, a copper!'

The Air Commodore rose. 'Go and see what you can cop,' he invited. 'Now I must be getting back. I'd like you to make a start as soon as possible, otherwise the regular operating companies will set up a scream. The public may jib at flying in machines that are liable to be shot down, and if they did we could hardly blame them. Goodbye for the present. Come and see me when you check in at the Yard.'

The Air Commodore went out to his car.

Chapter 2
Purely Technical

Biggles sat for some minutes deep in thought, watching the grey thread of smoke that rose from his cigarette to the ceiling.

'There's one point about this Raymond didn't mention,' he said slowly. 'You'll notice that all these jobs were directed against British concerns. The *Rajah* is a British ship, so the pearls would be insured with a British company. The diamonds were the property of the South African Government. Jaggersfontein Mining Concession, Limited, is a British company. Why pick on Britain?—or was that just a fluke? After all, other countries fly valuable freight, but apparently they have had no trouble. That these are no ordinary crooks we can judge by the size of the stuff they go for. They think in millions, and they've hit us a tidy crack already.'

'You mean, the bloke behind the scheme may have his knife into us, so that apart from the swag he has the satisfaction of revenge?' suggested Algy.

'It was just an idea,' returned Biggles thoughtfully. 'But let us for a start tackle the thing from the technical angle. That's our only advantage over the regular police. I can well understand that they don't know where to begin on a case like this. Normally, they rely largely on the type and method of the crime to give them a slant on the cracksman. But the man pulling

18

these jobs doesn't come into the category of common thief. He may not even have a police record. After all, think of the qualifications he must hold. He must be a first-class pilot, navigator, and mechanic.'

'A lot of fellows hold those qualifications today,' reminded Ginger.

'True enough,' agreed Biggles. 'But they do at least limit the possibilities. Men with those qualifications can earn good money. Most men turn crook when they can't pick up cash any other way. Why should this chap go off the rails? It comes back to the point I made just now. There is more behind this than mere money. The chap made a fortune out of his first crack—the pearls. Why does he go on?' Biggles lit another cigarette.

'We can line up one or two facts right away,' he resumed. 'One. This bloke has a base aerodrome. Two, it is hidden away in some remote place beyond the view of possible spectators. Remember, after a machine has taken off, while it is climbing for height, it can be seen from a long way round. Three, the chap has access to a considerable quantity of petrol and oil. He isn't getting it from a public airport, so he must have a private dump. We may assume that the landing-ground is near the dump—or vice versa.'

'And the dump might be anywhere on the face of the globe,' put in Algy cynically.

'I don't altogether agree with you there,' argued Biggles. 'Here again there are certain limitations—but we'll come back to that presently. I'm most interested in the aircraft. Forget the description of the unidentified plane reported by that sailor and run over those you know; by a process of elimination you'll soon see that there aren't many machines with the speed, range, and adaptability, of this particular kite*, which can hop from the Middle East to North America and from South Africa to South America. The plane may, or may not, have landed in America. It might have dropped the swag to an accomplice and flown straight back to its base. Much would depend, of course, on where it started from, but I can only think of two machines with such a performance.'

Algy stepped in. 'Our latest long-distance fighter, the Spur, which was just going into production when the war ended, has an outstanding range, so they say.'

'That's one of the two I had in mind,' acknowledged Biggles. 'But there is only one Spur, and that's still under test. Had it been pinched we should have heard about it. Apart from that, I visualise something larger, because there is reason to suppose that at least two or three men are engaged in this racket.'

'The Spur is a two-seater,' Algy pointed out.

'I know,' answered Biggles, 'but in this racket several specialised jobs are involved. First, there is the crew, although I admit that the pilot, navigator, and mechanic might be one man. It takes more than one to handle a heavy engine, though; I should say there are at least two airmen. Then there must be someone who knows the jewel trade pretty well. Not only would such a man be needed to dispose of the gems, but only a fellow who has had some association with the precious stone business would know about the pearl harvest in the Persian Gulf, and the times and method of transporting diamonds from Alexander Bay to Capetown.

*Slang: aircraft.

Then what about the safe in the *Rajah*? The back was cut out. It may have been an old safe, but that job couldn't have been done with a pair of pliers. It sounds more like the work of a professional crook, one who has handled safes before.'

'These people may be using more than one aircraft,' suggested Ginger. 'There is certainly a fighter, or a machine fitted with guns, in the party. Having done a job, say, in Africa, there would be no point in carrying guns and ammunition all the way to America. A transport plane could do that—unless the fighter returned to its base and dismantled its military equipment before going on to the States.'

Biggles nodded. 'There may be something in that,' he assented. 'In fact, that theory hooks up with the other machine—or rather, machines—I had in mind. Just before the war ended there was a rumour in the service—it must have leaked out from Intelligence, as these things do—that a new German designer named Renkell, Ludwig Renkell I think it was, had two red-hot jobs under test. From all accounts they were something super. One was a twin-engined two-seat fighter with some novel features that gave it an extraordinary turn of speed—both fast and slow. The other was a modification of the same type, also a twin-engined job, in the light bomber class, on the lines of our Mosquito, but slightly larger. They didn't get into production, but both prototypes whizzed through their tests—at least, so our agents reported. I wonder what happened to those machines? I should have thought our people would have taken them over, but come to think of it I haven't heard a word about them.'

'Why not ring old Freddie Lavers at Air Intelligence?'

suggested Bertie. 'He might know something about them.'

'I think I will.' Biggles reached for the phone and put the call through on the private wire.

'Is that you, Freddie?' he began. 'Biggles here. I want a spot of pukka gen* about those two super proto-types that rumour alleged were under test at Augsburg . . . a new bloke named Renkell designed them . . . yes . . . yes. Well, I'll go hopping!' Biggles fell silent, listening. Twice he threw a curious glance at the others. Occasionally he murmured, 'Ah-huh.' Finally, he said, 'Many thanks, Freddie. See you some-time. So long.' He hung up with irritating deliberation and turned slowly in his chair.

'What do you know about that?' he said softly. 'Both machines have disappeared. At any rate, our people haven't been able to lay hands on them. They say they can't be found. They had gone when our people arrived to take over the aerodrome. When questioned, the workmen just looked blank and said they knew nothing about such machines.'

'Something fishy about that, by Jove!' swore Bertie. 'Dirty work at the crossroads, and so on. What about the blue-prints?'

'They can't be found, either.' Biggles smiled, a pecul-iar smile. 'Neither can Renkell be found, or his test pilot, a chap named Baumer. Of course,' he went on quickly, 'it would be silly to jump to conclusions. Several machines disappeared from Germany after the last war** before we could get hold of them. One

*RAF slang: trustworthy information.
**World War I 1914–1918.

22

designer had the brass face to admit, some time afterwards, that he took his machines away because he considered that they were his personal property.'

'Absolute poppycock,' declared Bertie, polishing his eyeglass. 'They belonged to the German Government, so they should have been handed over to us.'

'Of course—but people are like that,' murmured Biggles dryly. 'To get back to the point, Freddie said that as far as he knew, Renkell was a genuine designer. He also said he knew nothing about Baumer except that before he became a test pilot he was with Rommel* in North Africa, and that he was pally with Julius Gontermann, the Nazi liaison officer between Hitler and the Luftwaffe.**'

'Surely Gontermann is one of the Nazis our people are still looking for?' said Algy quickly. 'He's wanted for crimes in Poland and Czechoslovakia. I read something about it in the paper within the last day or two.'

'I believe you're right,' returned Biggles quickly. 'Gontermann would know, or guess, that he was on our black list, so he was pretty certain to bolt when Germany cracked. If Baumer was a pal of his he might well ask him to fly him out of the country. If Baumer agreed, nothing would be more natural than for him to pinch the best machine in his charge—with or without Renkell's permission. They might have taken Renkell along with them.' Biggles shrugged. 'Of course, we may be barking up the wrong tree, but this is worth following up. I wonder where we could get particulars of

*General commanding the German armed forces in North Africa 1941–1943.
**The name of the German airforce from 1935 through World War II.

Gontermann's history and private life? Raymond would know, but he can't have got back to his office yet.'

'There was quite a piece about Gontermann in the paper I mentioned,' said Algy.

'What paper was it?'

'*The Times.*'

'Can you remember what it said?'

'I didn't read it,' admitted Algy. 'I just saw the headline, that's all.'

'The paper should be in the salvage bag, if it hasn't been collected. See if you can find it.'

Algy went off, and presently returned dragging a sack. 'I saw the notice within the last two or three days, so the paper should be near the top,' he announced. He picked up several newspapers and glanced at the dates. 'This should be it,' he went on, spreading a crumpled copy of *The Times* on the desk. He glanced through the pages. 'Here we are!' he cried. 'I'll read what it says:

'No news has yet been received concerning the whereabouts of the Nazi party chief, Gontermann, against whom there is a long list of indictments. Julius Hans Gontermann was born at Garlin, Mecklenburg, in 1902. He was destined for a military career, but as a cadet he was dismissed for some misdemeanour and went into politics. In this he was also unsuccessful, and was next heard of as an associate of Max Grindler, German-born Public Enemy No. 1 in the U.S.A. When Grindler was run down by G-men, Gontermann turned State's evidence and got off with a light sentence. On his release from prison he took up crime on his own account, specialising as a jewel smuggler between Europe and

24

America. For this, in 1930, he served a three years' sentence and was then deported. Returning to Germany he joined the Nazi party, and his subsequent advancement may have been due to a streak of ruthless cruelty which first manifested itself during the Spanish Civil War, when he was attached to the Condor Legion,* and later, in Czechoslovakia and Poland. In March 1942 he was decorated by Hitler with the Knight's Insignia of the Iron Cross for his work in the First Air Fleet under Generaloberst Keller, and was shortly afterwards promoted to Hitler's personal staff. Gontermann is good-looking, but tends to ostentation in his dress and manners.'

Algy looked up from the paper. 'That's all.'

'Well—well,' murmured Biggles. 'How very interesting. So Gontermann was a crook. There's an old tag, "once a crook always a crook". If he was attached to the Condor Legion in Spain he must know quite a bit about flying.'

'A pukka jail-bird, by jingo!' chuckled Bertie.

Biggles nodded. 'Baumer must have known about his murky record, which tars him with the same brush—otherwise he wouldn't have associated with him. Of course, there is still no hook-up between this bunch and the gang we're after, but we've got to start somewhere, and the Gontermann-Baumer alliance offers possibilities, if only on account of their combined quali-

*German Aircraft supporting the Nationalist and Fascist General Franco of Spain in his civil war with the Spanish government 1936–1939 which ended in victory for Franco, who had the support of Hitler.

fications. Even if they are not our birds we can safely assume that they're up to no good.'

'Where do we start looking for them, old warrior?' inquired Bertie.

'Suppose we start by eliminating the countries where they are *not* likely to be,' answered Biggles. 'If they've bolted out of Germany, and presumably they have, there aren't many countries where they'd be safe—certainly not in Europe. Gontermann would hardly dare to show his face in Spain, or any of the late occupied countries. Nazis are not popular even in Italy. Yet they would certainly have a definite objective, a parking-place, in mind, when they bolted, and it would not be unreasonable to suppose that it is a place where one of them has been before. In fact, the existence of a suitable hide-out may have led to the flight. They could only know of it from personal experience. But we may be going a bit too fast. I'll think this over while we're getting organised. Let's go to town. In the morning I'll go to the Air Ministry about equipment. We'll also inspect the new office Raymond has promised us. Then I think we'll take a trip.'

Ginger opened his eyes wide. 'A trip? To where?'

'To Germany,' replied Biggles. 'I think we'll start at Augsburg. That's where the Renkell prototypes started from. We might strike what, as policemen, we should call a clue.'

'Ha! Fingerprints and what-not?' murmured Bertie.

'Not exactly,' returned Biggles, smiling. 'Nowadays, even second-class crooks know better than to make such elementary blunders. Aside from that, it would hardly be surprising to find Renkell's fingerprints in his own works. But we may find something—and when

26

I say that I'm still thinking on technical lines. We've done enough guessing. Let's get along.'

Chapter 3
The Yellow Swan

The following afternoon two aeroplanes glided down to land on the aerodrome at Augsburg. Both were obviously military machines, although the identification markings were British civil registration letters. The faint outline of red and blue concentric rings could just be followed under a new coat of sombre grey. One machine was a Mosquito*, a type that had become famous during the war for its daylight skip-bombing** raids. The other was the Spur, a twin-engined, two-seat, high-performance fighter that was only prevented from making history by the termination of the war. Together, the two aircraft taxied to the control building. From the Spur emerged Biggles and Ginger. Algy and Bertie dropped from the Mosquito and joined them. All wore civilian clothes. There had been some discussion as to whether they should all go to Germany. Biggles had pointed out that four made a large party, but in the end he had decided to take the two machines, the Mosquito being in the nature of a 'spare' should one be needed.

*British De Havilland twin-engined fighter bomber with a crew of two and a top speed of 400 mph. Armed with four 20 mm cannon and four machine guns.
**A method of bombing by releasing bombs from a very low altitude, making the bombs glance off the surface of the ground or water and skip along horizontally with the ground until they hit their target.

On the way to the office he paused for a moment to indicate a group of buildings on the right. 'Those are Willy Messerschmitt's works,*' he observed. 'Those on the left must be the new Renkell outfit. They weren't here the last time I came over.' He walked on until he was halted by an R.A.F. sergeant who inquired his business.

'Detective-sergeant Bigglesworth, of the C.I.D., to see Wing Commander Howath,' answered Biggles.

'This way, sir,' said the sergeant. 'The Wing Commander is expecting you.' He led the way to a room where an officer in R.A.F. blue, wearing the badges of rank of a wing commander, was sorting out some papers.

Smiling, the wing commander held out his hand in greeting. 'Hello, Biggles. What the devil's all this about?' he asked. 'I got a signal from the Air House to say you were on the way. They tell me you've gone over to the police force, to try to recover some jewels or something. It should be rather fun, if they pay you well—'

'The bloke at the Air House who told you that has got the wrong idea,' interrupted Biggles coldly. 'At the moment my new job is neither funny or profitable; but if I am successful I shall get more out of it than amusement and cash. You see, some people have been murdered, two pilots among them. I didn't know these chaps, but as they were in the same line of business as ourselves something ought to be done about it. I know that murder, to most people who like to read about it, means a gory body in a dismal cellar. Being shot down

*Highly successful German aircraft manufacturer during World War II.

in an aircraft may lack the blood-curdling thrill of throat-cutting on a dark night, but it's murder just the same. In this case the murderer shot his unsuspecting victims through the back, which makes it worse. I aim to catch this skunk. That's all. Now let's get on.'

'Sorry,' muttered the wing commander contritely, his eyes on Biggles's face. 'Sit down. Have a cigarette? What can I do for you?'

'I'm looking for the Renkell prototypes,' answered Biggles bluntly.

'You won't find them here,' asserted the wing commander. 'They've gone—if they ever existed.'

Biggles looked up sharply. 'What do you mean—if they ever existed? Are you suggesting that our Intelligence people were talking through their hats?'

'Er—no—not exactly,' answered the wing commander, awkwardly.

'Sounded like it to me,' returned Biggles. 'Either the machines exist, or they do not. Intelligence say they do, and that's good enough for me.'

'Okay. Go ahead and find them,' invited the wing commander. 'All I can tell you is, there's no trace of them here. We made a thorough search. First thing we looked for.'

'What about the workmen? What have they to say?'

'Most of them had gone by the time we got here. A few stayed on. I questioned them. They say they know nothing about such machines. They admit Renkell was working on new types, but swear they never got beyond the drawing-board.'

'What are these men doing now?'

'Just looking after things, presumably.'

'Who pays them?'

The wing commander raised his eyebrows. 'I've never inquired. It's no business of mine. The works manager pays them, I suppose.'

'Who pays the works manager?'

'How the hell should I know? I've never asked him. I've only spoken to him once. He told me they were turning over the plant to light plane production. He's got a machine of his own in the shed—useful-looking job.'

'Then this chap is a pilot?'

'Yes. He served in the Boelcke staffel* in nineteen-eighteen. Says he was too old for war flying in the last fuss.'

'What's this man's name?'

'Preuss—Rudolf Preuss.'

'What sort of fellow is he?'

The wing commander frowned. 'Look here, Biggles, the Ministry told me to give you all the assistance possible, but aren't you flogging a dead horse?'

'I've nothing else to flog at the moment,' answered Biggles imperturbably. 'Tell me about this fellow Preuss.'

The wing commander shrugged. 'He's a typical Prussian, I should say. About forty-five—tall, flaxen, blue-eyed, stalwart type, has one of those aggressive moustaches. Efficient-looking bloke.'

'Where can he be found?'

'Either in the works, or in his office.'

---

*Oswald Boelcke was one of the leading German fighter Aces of World War I with forty victories. A German staffel is the equivalent of a British squadron, and was often known by the name of its leader. It is also sometimes called a jagdstaffel.

Biggles rose. 'I'd like a word with him. By the way, you haven't mentioned to anyone why I'm here?'

'No.'

'Please don't. You can give it out that I'm a British manufacturer with his technical staff having a look round for likely types to build under licence.'

'As you say. Like me to come with you?'

'That's not a bad idea. You can introduce us. After that, leave the talking to me.'

The wing commander put on his cap and led the way to the Renkell works.

They found Preuss in his office, and saw at a glance that the wing commander had given a fair description of the man. His manner, when the introductions were effected, was curt to the point of rudeness, but Biggles took no notice. It was understandable. After an exchange of formalities Biggles asked, casually, 'What happened to the two prototypes you had here?'

Preuss stiffened. 'I have already made a report. There are no such machines,' he said harshly, in good English. 'I am the manager. I should know.'

'What were you building when the war ended?' asked Biggles.

'Seeing the end of the war in sight, Herr Renkell was developing a civil type, in the light plane class.'

'In that case, why did Renkell leave?'

'He did not tell me,' sneered the German sarcastically.

Biggles nodded. 'I see. We'll have a look round while we're here if you don't mind?'

'The works have already been examined,' said Preuss, in a surly voice.

'Look, Preuss, I understand how you feel about this,'

replied Biggles quietly. 'But I've come a long way, and I might as well see what there is to be seen. You can stay here and talk to Wing Commander Howath. We'll find our own way round.' Biggles beckoned to the others, who followed him out into the corridor. He closed the door.

'Bad-tempered cuss,' muttered Algy.

Biggles did not answer. He had stopped before a door marked private. Under the word was the name, Kurt Baumer. 'This must have been the test pilot's office,' he said softly, as he tried the handle. The door opened and he went in.

There was little to see. It was evident that the room was no longer used. Only the furniture remained. The cupboard was empty, as was the locker. Biggles tried the desk. That, too, had been thoroughly cleared. The only paper in the room was in the waste-paper basket. Biggles emptied it on the desk and ran through the contents—one or two old newspapers, some blank forms, and a few odds and ends. Two screwed up pieces of paper turned out to be bills, both from tailors in Augsburg. Lying together were several snapshots of a Messerschmitt, in each case the same machine.

'That must have been Baumer's war-horse,' observed Biggles. 'That's probably him in the cockpit, but it's too small to give us much idea of what he looked like. I'll keep one and have it enlarged when we get back. Hallo, what's this?'

He had picked up another snapshot, this one a head and shoulders of a saturnine young man in Italian Air Force uniform. On the back a few words had been written in Italian. Biggles translated, reading aloud:

'Souvenir of good comradeship, Libya, 1941. To Kurt, from his friend, Carlos Scaroni. Escadrille 33.'

'Hm. Baumer must have got thick with this fellow Scaroni when he was in Libya with Rommel,' went on Biggles. 'It seems likely that they served on the same aerodrome, since they got to know each other so well. It may mean nothing, but we'll remember it.' He put the photo in his pocket, swept the other papers into the basket and replaced it in its original position. 'Now let's have a look at the works,' he suggested.

When they entered the machine shop some half a dozen men were standing together, talking; they fell silent when the newcomers entered. Biggles nodded to them and then strolled on through the workshop, his eyes taking in every detail. They were the usual lathes and presses, but nothing unusual. He examined several of the presses. 'These are all new jigs and patterns,' he said quietly. 'It's no use asking Preuss what they were using before these were put in. We shan't find anything here—the place has been cleaned up. Let's try the scrap-heap; there's bound to be one. If I know anything about aerodromes it will be at the back of the hangar.'

Leaving the workshops they went on to the rear of the one large hangar, where, as Biggles had predicted, they found the usual accumulation of waste material—fabric, timber, and both sheet and tubular metal. Biggles turned over several pieces.

'Take a look,' he said grimly. 'Nearly all this stuff has been flattened under a press. Why should they go to that trouble? You can guess the answer. Preuss is thorough all right, but here he has gone too far. The fact that he has been to the expense of smashing everything makes it quite certain that he had something to hide.' Stooping, he pulled out a flattened mass of tubular metal. 'Straighten that out between you, and see what it looks like,' he ordered.

Leaving them to the task he went on delving into the pile, and presently drew out a short length of steel tubing that had escaped the press. Then a cry from Algy brought him round. Looking, he saw that the tubing had taken rough shape. It now formed the rough outline of a rudder. The shape was nearly oval.

Biggles whistled softly. 'By thunder!' he exclaimed. 'An oval rudder. That sailor who spotted the machine crossing the South Atlantic was right. This stuff must have been the original mock-up*. All right. We've seen enough. Buckle it up and throw it back. Look at this piece of tubing I've found. No aircraft, even a heavy bomber, has longerons that size. It could only be one thing—a boom. This is a piece cut off it. That sailor was certainly right in his description. We haven't wasted our time after all. One of those prototypes, if not both, crossed the Atlantic. Whether it's still there or not is another matter. Let's see what's in the hangar.'

As they entered the big building, occupied by a single aircraft, a small civil type painted an ugly ochre yellow without registration marks of any sort, Preuss appeared, walking quickly. His face was slightly flushed.

'Hello, I thought you were with Wing Commander Howath,' said Biggles easily.

'He has returned to his office,' snapped Preuss. 'This

---

*Before a new type of aircraft is built, a rough, non-flying, full-sized model is made from the drawings, to give an idea of what the machine will look like, and to enable adjustments to be made, where necessary. This is called a mock-up.

is not a military machine. It is a private plane. What are you doing?'

Biggles shrugged. 'We've hardly had time to look at it. This is your machine, I understand?'

'Yes, it is mine,' assented Preuss in a hard voice.

'Mind if I have a look at it?'

'You won the war, so I suppose you can do what you like,' almost spat the German.

Biggles's expression did not change. 'Talking in that strain won't help to mend our differences,' he said evenly. 'If you must talk about the war, you should remember who started it. But let us not go into that.' He turned back to the machine. 'This is one of Herr Renkell's designs, I imagine?'

'What makes you think that?' asked Preuss sourly.

'Because designers tend to adhere to certain fixed ideas, with the result that their products usually have one or more features in common. That applies particularly to tail structures. One can tell who designed almost any machine by the shape of its tail—as you probably know. The rudder of this machine of yours is nearly oval. I gather that Mr. Renkell is partial to that shape?'

Preuss was staring hard at Biggles. 'Where did you see one of Herr Renkell's machines?' he inquired, with venom in his voice.

Biggles puckered his forehead. 'I can't remember. Perhaps someone described one to me.'

Preuss did not answer.

Biggles walked up to the machine, opened the cabin door and surveyed the interior. He invited the others to look. 'You must admit that the Germans are thorough,' he remarked. 'Take a look at that instrument panel. They've worked in every conceivable gadget. Roomy cabin, too.' He glanced over his shoulder. 'You've installed a big petrol tank for a light plane, haven't you?' he inquired.

'We take the view that long range will be demanded by private owners,' answered Preuss. 'If one has to keep landing to pick up fuel, paying landing fees every time, private flying will be expensive.'

'That sounds a reasonable argument,' agreed Biggles. 'Presumably you're thinking of putting this type on the market?'

'After some modifications have been made,' returned Preuss. 'As usual with a new type, there are teething troubles. The plane is still in the experimental stage. We are not ready to sell.'

Biggles nodded. 'I see.' He closed the cabin door. 'Let me know when you're putting the machine on the market,' he requested.

'Very well.'

'Tell me,' went on Biggles, pointing to a name that had been painted on the engine cowling, 'why did you call this machine Swan, and then paint it that dirty yellow?'

Preuss hesitated. 'It can be painted any colour,' he answered.

'That's true,' agreed Biggles carelessly. 'Well, I think that's about all. We'll be getting along. Good afternoon, Mr. Preuss.'

The German bowed stiffly.

Leaving him in the hangar Biggles walked towards the control office. For a little while he was silent, deep in thought. Then he said, 'There are points about that machine that excite my curiosity. To start with, if it

37

was intended for a private owner, as Preuss asserts, the price would limit sales. I doubt if it could be turned out under a couple of thousand pounds, and not many people have that amount of money to spend on what is still a luxury vehicle.'

'The price could be dropped by discarding some of the equipment,' Algy pointed out.

'Then why install it in the first place?' argued Biggles. 'What about that main tank? With all due respect to the plausible Mr. Preuss, few private owners would demand a range of two thousand miles. His argument about economy in the matter of landing fees is bunk. It would be cheaper to pay a landing fee here and there than haul that weight of petrol around. No, I can't accept that.'

'What did you mean by that crack about the dirty colour?' asked Bertie.

'It would be hard to think of a more unbecoming colour for a private plane,' answered Biggles. 'It was certainly not put on for appearance. If it was not put on for appearance then it must have been for a purpose. I can think of only one purpose. They painted planes, and tanks, that colour, for the Libyan campaign, to make them hard to see against the sand. Baumer served in Libya. Unless I'm mistaken we're going to have desert sand gritting in our teeth before this job's over. I'll tell you another thing about Mr. Preuss's Swan. With all that equipment he forgot something really necessary. Radio. Or did he forget? Did you notice the thickness of that bulkhead? Did you ever know a designer to pack in unnecessary weight like that? I never did. There's something in that bulkhead. I should say it's radio. Why hide it? There may be a good reason, but the one that comes to my mind is, because like everything else in that machine, it is a more efficient and expensive outfit than the type could possibly warrant. The more I think about it, the more convinced I am that that kite was never intended for the popular market. The original conception might have been—but not that machine.'

'You think Preuss is in the Gontermann-Baumer plot?' queried Algy.

'If he's not actually in the scheme I'm pretty sure he knows where the missing machines are,' returned Biggles. 'Gontermann and Baumer would need an inconspicuous communication aircraft to keep them in touch with things at home, and that bilious-looking Swan could do the job very well. It would be interesting to know, too, who is paying Preuss to keep the works running now the boss has disappeared. We'll keep an eye on this bird.'

Biggles went into the office.

Chapter 4
Preuss Plays A Card

The Wing Commander was putting on his cap. 'Find anything?' he asked cheerfully.

'Nothing to speak of,' answered Biggles, cautiously. 'What time do you usually knock off work?'

'About four-thirty. It's that now. I'm just going.'

'Where are you staying?'

'I've got quarters in the town—at the Colon Hotel.'

'How about your lads, the care and maintenance party?'

'They live in billets round the aerodrome.'

'Do they knock off when you go?'

'Yes, usually.'

'I see. So after four-thirty there's no supervision here?'

'That's right. There's really nothing for us to do, you know, now we've finished taking an inventory of the place. We shall probably be withdrawn altogether very soon. Are you chaps going back to London?'

'I haven't made up my mind yet,' averred Biggles.

'There's plenty of room in the hangars for your machines, if you want to stay.'

'Thanks. I'll decide later. Don't let us keep you.'

'All right. If you don't need me I'll push along. Leave the key of the office with the sergeant.' With a nod the Wing Commander departed.

40

'If we are going back to England we can just do it in daylight, if we start fairly soon,' Algy pointed out.

Biggles did not answer. He was staring through the window. Suddenly he made a dash for the door. He did not speak.

After a startled glance the others followed, wondering what had happened. By the time they were outside Biggles was walking briskly along the tarmac to intercept a man in workman's overalls who had just left the vicinity of the two British aircraft. The man, a small, dark, ill-nourished-looking fellow in the early twenties, saw him coming, and quickened his pace; but Biggles overtook him.

'Just a minute,' he said, speaking in German.

The man stopped, glancing apprehensively in the direction of the Renkell works.

'What were you doing over there by those machines?' asked Biggles curtly.

'I was just looking at them, sir,' answered the man, nervously.

'Are you one of Mr. Preuss's men?'

'Yes.'

'So you're interested in flying, eh?'

'Of course.'

'Good. I always like to encourage young fellows who are interested,' said Biggles pleasantly. 'Come on, I'll take you up.'

The man did not move.

'What's the matter—don't you want a joy-ride?' asked Biggles.

The man moistened his lips, and glanced again at the works. 'No,' he blurted.

Biggles's manner changed. 'What have you been up

41

to?' he asked crisply, his eyes on a pair of pliers that projected from the man's pocket.

'Nothing.'

'In that case a joy-ride won't hurt you.' Biggles took the man firmly by the arm. 'Come on.'

Protesting, the man was taken to the Spur.

'Get in,' ordered Biggles grimly.

The man hung back. His face was white. Beads of sweat were standing on his forehead. 'No—no!' he cried.

'But I say yes,' rasped Biggles, thrusting the man towards the machine. 'I am going to fly this aircraft and you're coming with me.'

Again the man's tongue flicked over his lips. 'No,' he panted.

'Why not? Not nervous are you?'

'We—I—we should both be killed.'

'Ah!' breathed Biggles. 'I thought so. What did you do? Speak up.'

The man's breath was coming fast. Clearly, he was badly scared. 'I cut the aileron control,*' he gasped.

'Why did you do that? Come on, let's have the truth or I'll have you sent to prison for life, for sabotage and attempted murder,' promised Biggles. 'Why did you try to kill me?'

'I didn't want to do it—I swear I didn't,' pleaded the wretched man, whose nerves seemed to have gone to pieces.

'Then why did you?'

*A hinged control surface set into or near the rear edge of an aircraft wing and used to maintain the rolling movements of the aircraft. Ailerons work in pairs: one side lifting up while the other stays down and the resulting 'pull' allows the aircraft to bank or turn.

'He made me.'

'Who made you?'

'Herr Preuss. For God's sake don't tell him I told you or he'll kill me.' The man's terror was almost pathetic.

'So you're afraid of Preuss?' Biggles's remark was more a statement than a question.

'He's a man to be afraid of,' was the answer.

'I see. Well, having gone so far you might as well make a clean breast of the rest. Where are the two machines that disappeared from here?'

'I don't know, and that's God's truth, sir,' declared the German.

'But they *were* here?'

The man betrayed himself by hesitation.

'Come on—I'm waiting,' snapped Biggles.

'Heaven help me if Preuss ever finds out I told you,' moaned the man. 'Yes, they were here. I helped to build them.'

'A fighter and a light bomber?'

'Yes.'

'What's your trade—fitter?'

'Yes.'

'Did you help to fit the undercarriages?'

'Yes.'

'Then you'd know the dimension of the wheel track of the bomber?'

'It was four metres. I didn't fit the Wolf—that's what they call the fighter—but it was slightly less.'

'Where did these machines go?'

'I don't know. I wasn't told. I don't think anyone knew except Preuss. He and Herr Baumer were always whispering together.'

'So Baumer flew one of the machines?'

'Yes.'

'Who went in the party?'

'There were five of them. The machines went together, at night. The only people I knew were Renkell and Baumer. Herr Renkell seemed upset. Baumer flew the fighter, taking Herr Renkell with him.'

'What about the bomber?'

'It has been converted into a transport. I didn't know the man who flew it. He only arrived the day before. I think he was an Italian. Baumer called him Carlos.'

Biggles glanced at Algy before continuing. 'Who were the passengers?'

'From pictures I've seen of him I think one was Herr Gontermann. The other was a stranger, an American by his accent. He— But here comes Herr Preuss. He's seen me talking to you. For God's sake don't let him know what I've told you.'

'All right. You can trust me,' promised Biggles. 'It will be worth your while to do so. Tell me this. Preuss saw the two machines off, eh?'

'Yes.'

'What's your name?'

'Schneider—Franz Schneider.'

'Where can I find you if I want you? Preuss is heading for trouble, so if you want to keep out of the mess you'd better be honest.'

'I live at number forty Unterstrasse, Augsburg. I have a room on the top floor.'

'If Preuss attempts to leave the ground in his machine, I want you to ring me up at once and let me know. We've no time for more now. Get in touch with me at the Colon Hotel and we'll fix an appointment. Ask for Sergeant Bigglesworth.'

'Yes, sir.'

Preuss came hurrying up, his expression heavy with suspicion. 'What's the matter here?' he demanded.

'Nothing to get upset about, surely,' returned Biggles calmly. 'This lad was interested in my machine. I was telling him a few things about it. Any objection?'

'I don't like my staff talking with strangers,' said Preuss brusquely. 'Get back to your work, Schneider.'

The mechanic walked off, looking servile in the presence of a superior.

'Anything else you want to say, Mr. Preuss?' asked Biggles quietly.

'No.'

'Then don't let us keep you.'

Preuss clicked his heels, bowed, and departed.

With a pensive expression in his eyes Biggles watched him go. 'A typical bullying Nazi, if ever there was one,' he observed. 'A potential murderer, at that. He sent that lad to sabotage the plane. Lucky I spotted him, otherwise we should have scattered ourselves all over the aerodrome when we tried to take off. Preuss knows what we're after. I fancy there's more in this affair than ever Raymond suspects. A dangerous type, is Mr. Preuss. He'll watch us from his office. When he sees us repairing that severed cable he'll know his plan for bumping us off has failed. I imagine he'll let Gontermann and Co. know that we're around. One thing is certain. We couldn't get back to England before dark even if we wanted to—and I'm not sure that I want to. I'd like another word with that fellow Schneider. He has no stomach for this job, and he's ready to talk, to save himself. He's scared stiff of Preuss, there's no doubt about that.'

'You told Schneider you'd be at the Colon,' reminded Ginger.

'I spoke on the spur of the moment, but I think I will stay there,' answered Biggles. 'We'll get the Spur into one of the empty hangars and repair the damage. Algy, you'd better have a good look round your machine, too. I've got a little job for you and Bertie.'

'Have you, by Jove?' murmured Bertie. 'What is it?'

'I want you to take a quick trip to the Persian Gulf,' answered Biggles casually.

Algy started. 'To *where*?'

'You heard me.'

'What's the idea?'

Biggles lit a cigarette. 'Because it's the thing to do,' he went on, smiling faintly. 'If murder novels and cinema thrillers are to be believed, the first thing the best detectives do is visit the scene of the crime. The first crime of our series was the pearl robbery in the Persian Gulf. I didn't rush straight off there, but had we drawn blank here I should have had a look round. We now have something definite to look for. Somehow—it doesn't matter how—the man who pinched the pearls left the *Rajah* and reached the coast, where a plane must have been waiting to take the swag to America. Naturally, the plane would wait on the side of the Gulf nearest to America. That's Arabia. I doubt if a plane could land on the other side, the Persian side, anyway, because it's mostly cliff and rock. The Arabian coast is flat sand. You could put a machine down almost anywhere, but you couldn't do it without leaving wheel marks.'

'But just a minute, old boy,' put in Bertie. 'If Baumer is as smart as he seems to be, he might have erased the tracks after he landed.'

'So he might,' agreed Biggles. 'But he'd be a thunderingly clever man to erase the tracks he made taking off..The machine took off again after picking up the pearl thief.'

Bertie made a gesture of disgust. 'What a bally idiot I am. Never thought of that, by jingo. You're absolutely right.'

'As I was saying,' went on Biggles, 'unless there has been a sand-storm, somewhere along that coast there are wheel tracks. There's no likelihood of their being obliterated by traffic because there isn't any traffic. It's Arab country, and most of the Arabs are in the towns— and there aren't many towns, anyway. I don't suppose anyone walks that coast once in a blue moon. I want you to go down and find the tracks. Cruise along the coast, low. On that unbroken sand, tyre marks should stand out like tank traps. Having found what you're looking for, land, measure the wheel tracks carefully, and then come home. Those tracks can tell us a lot, which is why I asked Schneider about them. He says the wheel track of the Renkell bomber—or, rather, transport—is four metres. That's a trifle over thirteen feet—thirteen feet one and a half inches, to be precise, if I haven't forgotten my arithmetic. If you find two grooves in the sand thirteen feet apart we shall know where the Gontermann-Baumer syndicate went when it bolted from here, and why. You've a longish hop in front of you—close on three thousand miles the way you'll have to go—so you'd better get cracking. If I were you I'd go via Malta and Alexandria, so that you can pick up petrol at R.A.F. stations. By taking turns at the controls you ought to be able to run right through. You should be at Basra, at the head of the Gulf, about dawn. Have a rest and a bite while the boys are servicing the machine, then go on. Unless you get a signal from me at Alex or Malta on the way back, go straight home to Croydon. Unless something happens in the meantime I shall be there myself by then.'

Algy nodded. 'Okay. We'll get off right away. Watch your step with Preuss. He's a nasty piece of work. Come on, Bertie.'

Then went out, leaving Biggles and Ginger alone.

'You get busy on that repair job,' ordered Biggles. 'I'll ring Howath and ask him to mount a guard over the aircraft all night. I don't feel like giving Preuss a second chance to try any funny tricks. I'll ask Howath to book a couple of rooms at the Colon at the same time. We'll sleep there tonight. After dinner we'll try to get in touch with Schneider. I fancy he knows more than he had time to tell us. Even if this Renkell gang was not responsible for the robberies the authorities will be glad to have information about them. They're up to something, and it's something pretty big. If Schneider is to be believed, and I feel pretty sure he was telling the truth, there are at least six of them in it— Renkell, Gontermann, Baumer, Preuss, Carlos the Italian, and an unknown American. Carlos must be Carlos Scaroni, Baumer's pal, the chap who inscribed the photograph we found in Baumer's office. But how an American comes into it is a puzzler.'

'And that isn't the only thing that puzzles me,' remarked Ginger. 'How are we going to arrest six men, even if we find them? Suppose we did—what then? Even if they are engaged in skyway robbery, how the deuce are we going to prove it? If we found them tomorrow, what evidence should we have against them? How are you going to get evidence? How can you prove that a plane went to any particular place, when it leaves no trail in the air?'

'The ideal thing would be to catch them red-handed at something,' returned Biggles thoughtfully.

'But in that case they'd be in the air,' argued Ginger. 'You can stop a surface vehicle without hurting the occupants, but you can't stop a plane forcibly without knocking it down and killing the passengers. Should we be justified in doing that?'

'I don't know,' admitted Biggles. 'Raymond doesn't know, either. I asked him that very question. He said something about challenging, and shooting if the plane refused to go down.'

'Challenging? That implies the use of radio. You can't talk to another machine any other way. While we were requesting them to put their wheels on the ground they'd probably be popping at us with their guns. Shoot first and challenge afterwards, I should say.'

'The whole of this air business bristles with difficulties,' asserted Biggles. 'There will have to be new legislation to deal with it; until there is, we shall just have to use our discretion. There's nothing else we can do, as far as I can see.'

'If this chap Preuss is a sample of what we're up against, I'm glad we brought our automatics,*' declared Ginger.

*Pistols.

49

'I had a feeling we might need them,' murmured Biggles. 'But this won't do. Push on with the job. I'll give you a hand as soon as I've spoken to Howath.'

Chapter 5
Preuss Tries Again

Later in the evening, Biggles and Ginger were just sitting down to dinner in the Colon Hotel when a waiter informed Biggles that he was wanted on the telephone.

Biggles put down his napkin. 'That'll be Schneider,' he said softly to Ginger, and followed the waiter to the instrument.

He was away about twenty minutes. When he came back his manner was alert. 'Schneider,' he said quietly, in reply to Ginger's questioning glance, as he dropped into his chair. 'Things are moving fast. Preuss has had his machine pulled out and filled up for a long trip. He hasn't left the ground yet, but he's all set to go. If it were daylight I'd try to shadow him, but it's no use trying to follow him in the dark. I've done a deal with Schneider. The poor little devil is scared stiff of Preuss, and of this crooked business he's engaged in. He's afraid Preuss suspects he told us more than he should this afternoon. Before he would tell me anything he asked me to give him a thousand marks, which would, he said, enable him to clear off to another town and find a new job.'

'Did you say you would?'

'Yes. It seemed a reasonable request. I told him he could come here to collect the money at eight o'clock; we shall have finished eating by then. He said he'd come. He had something on his mind that he daren't say over the phone, but he told me a few things. Preuss has been away twice before, taking a fairly heavy load with him. On each occasion he left here overnight, with a full tank, heading south, and arrived back from that direction at dawn, with a nearly dry tank, looking as though he had been up all night. Schneider doesn't know where he went; as far as he knows, Preuss told no one; but if he headed south he must have gone to Italy, or North Africa.'

'He couldn't have got to North Africa and back without refuelling,' put in Ginger.

'There might have been petrol available at the other end,' returned Biggles. 'Let's work it out. The Swan can probably kick the air behind it at around two-fifty miles an hour. Preuss was away twelve hours. Allowing an hour at the objective he could have covered getting on for three thousand miles. Beyond that, it's guess-work.'

'Where the deuce does he get so much petrol at this end?' demanded Ginger.

'I asked Schneider that. He says there's a concrete underground tank near the top end of the Renkell hangar. The valve is under a pile of rubbish. It was put in by the Nazis—emergency war stores. Preuss should have declared it to Howath, but he didn't. He told the staff to keep their mouths shut about it.'

'We could collar him for that.'

'It wouldn't do us any good. I'd rather Preuss were free. We shall learn more from him that way than by locking him up. Now we know where Preuss gets his petrol at this end, we could at any time keep the Swan on the ground by seizing the petrol—but I don't think the time is quite ripe for that.'

'Did Schneider tell you anything else?'

'Very little. He got on the phone as quickly as possible to let me know about Preuss going off. It looks more and more as if the Swan is running a private communication line between Gontermann and Co. and Germany.'

'Did it take Schneider twenty minutes to tell you what you've just told me?' asked Ginger incredulously.

'No, as a matter of fact it didn't. After he had finished I put a call through to the Yard. I managed to get hold of Raymond, and asked him to do one or two things for me.'

'Such as?'

'For one thing I asked him to get the B.B.C. to keep an ear to the air for unofficial signals. I told him I was particularly interested in Southern Europe and North Africa. He said he thought he could get service operators at Malta and Alexandria to listen, too.'

'Didn't he wonder what you were up to?'

'Probably. But Raymond knows me too well to waste time asking premature questions. He was a bit shaken though, judging from his voice, when I asked him to query the United States Federal Bureau if Max Grindler was at large.'

Ginger started. 'Grindler!'

'Grindler, you remember, was the big-shot gangster with whom Gontermann worked when he was in the States.'

'But Gontermann squealed when Grindler was caught. Judging from what I've seen on the flicks, and read in the papers, American racketeers take a poor view of that sort of thing. Grindler's only reason for contacting Gontermann would be to bump him off.' Ginger spoke with warmth.

Biggles nodded assent. 'I agree. But according to Schneider, there's an American in this party over here, and Grindler is the only American crook who, as far as we know, has been associated with Gontermann or his confederates. Of course, it might be another member of the Grindler gang, but we've no way of checking up on that. We can check up on Grindler. It's a shot in the dark, but I thought it was worth trying.'

'From the way you speak of Gontermann and Co., although the machines belonged to Renkell I take it you regard Gontermann as the head of this thing?'

'I should say he's the boss by now, if he wasn't at the beginning. Gontermann is that sort of man. He'd have to be, to get as high as he did in the Nazi party. I can't imagine him taking orders from Renkell, or Baumer, or this Italian, Scaroni. By the way, I also asked Raymond to try to get particulars of Scaroni, and his unit, which from the photo seems to have been Escadrille* Thirty-three. He said he thought he could, although it might take a little time, because it would mean getting in touch with the Italian Record Office.' Biggles glanced at the clock. 'It's nearly eight. Schneider should be along any minute now. When he comes we'll ask him to join us over coffee. That should make him feel at home. I confess to some curiosity about this item of news he daren't mention over the phone.'

Another quarter of an hour passed. Biggles began to fidget.

•

*French: squadron.

'He's late,' he remarked, with a trace of anxiety in his voice. 'We'd better order some more coffee—this is nearly cold.'

Very soon he was looking at the clock every few minutes. At twenty past eight he left the dining-room, taking Ginger with him, and went into the vestibule, finding a seat that commanded a view of the swing doors. Still there was no sign of Schneider.

At eight-thirty Biggles got up. 'I don't like this,' he said bluntly. 'It begins to look as if he isn't coming.'

'Perhaps he's changed his mind,' suggested Ginger.

'A man in Schneider's position doesn't change his mind when there is a sum of money to be collected,' answered Biggles. 'I'm going to find out what's happened. We can leave word with the hall porter that if Schneider comes he is to wait. Let's go.'

A taxi not being available, a horse-cab took them to the Unterstrasse, which turned out to be an insalubrious thoroughfare in a poor quarter of the town. Biggles asked to be put down at the corner, where he paid the cab and dismissed it. Then he walked along the pavement, checking the numbers on the doors.

It did not take long to find number forty, which turned out to be a tall apartment house. The door stood ajar, revealing in the light of a dusty electric globe, a stone-paved hall, cold, dreary, depressing. There was no janitor.

'He said his room was on the top floor,' reminded Ginger.

'Let's go up.'

Biggles led the way up four flights of stone stairs. There they ended. There were two doors, one on either side of the landing. One stood ajar, as if the room was unoccupied. Ginger struck a match and saw that the other door was closed. On it a piece of pasteboard had been fastened with two drawing-pins. He held the match close, to see more clearly a name that had been written on it in block letters. 'F. Schneider,' he read aloud. 'This is it.'

Biggles knocked quietly on the door.

There was no reply.

He knocked again, louder.

Still no reply.

'He's out, apparently,' remarked Ginger. 'Probably gone round to the hotel.'

'No,' replied Biggles in a hard voice. 'At any rate, someone is inside—or has been. There's a light shining through the keyhole. That means there's no key in the lock. Why not, I wonder? Schneider didn't strike me as the sort of chap to live in a room that he couldn't lock.' As he finished speaking he reached for the handle, turned it, and pushed the door open.

For a moment he remained motionless, rigid, staring first at something that lay on the floor, then at a chaos of overturned furniture, or as much of it as could be seen in the feeble light of the candle that stood on a draining-board beside the sink.

'Good God! What a mess,' he breathed, and stepped into the room. 'Careful—don't touch anything,' he said in a brittle voice to Ginger, who followed him.

There was no need for Ginger to ask what had caused Biggles to exclaim. Across the floor lay a man in an attitude so shockingly grotesque that it could only mean one thing. The knees were drawn up into the stomach, and the hands were raised, with fingers bent like claws, as if to protect the face. The head rested in a pool of blood. Blood was everywhere. It had even splashed on the whitewashed ceiling.

Something inside Ginger seemed to freeze, yet, impelled by a horrid fascination, he took another pace forward and looked down at the face. One glance at the bared teeth and staring eyes settled any hope that the man might still be alive. It was Schneider, although he was only just recognisable.

'Poor little devil,' said Biggles grimly. 'He put up a fight for it, but he hadn't a hope against a brute the size of Preuss. Admittedly, I don't see anything to indicate that Preuss was the murderer, but knowing what we know, I haven't any doubt about it. Preuss must have been suspicious, and followed him—followed him to the phone, no doubt, and then back here. Schneider's fears were justified. Whether Preuss overheard the telephone conversation or not is something we are never likely to know, but he must have been pretty sure that Schneider had squealed to make a mess like this. Only a man blind with rage batters another man's brains out. Killing wasn't enough. Schneider's head is smashed to pulp. Preuss must have gone on bashing him after he was dead. No wonder Schneider was scared of his boss; he knew him better than we did.'

'We know now,' murmured Ginger.

Biggles nodded. 'I shan't forget it, either.' He glanced round the room. 'I don't see the weapon, so the murderer must have taken it away with him. It must have been something pretty heavy, a tool, probably—a hammer, or spanner, or something of the sort. Well, it's not much use staying here. We shall never learn from Schneider what it was he wanted to tell us. Let's get out of this shambles.'

'Just a minute!' cried Ginger sharply. 'I think he's got something in his hand.'

Stooping, Biggles disengaged a small object from the fingers of the dead man's right hand. 'Hair,' he said. 'Fair hair. Quite a tuft. He must have torn it from his assailant's scalp in the struggle.'

'That supports the Preuss theory,' said Ginger. 'His hair is fair.'

'So is the hair of several million other Germans,' Biggles pointed out. 'If it did come from Preuss's head it must have been from the front, because if I remember rightly the back is close-cropped, Nazi style.'

'Are you going to take that hair away with you as evidence, or hand it over to the police?' inquired Ginger.

'Neither,' answered Biggles. 'I've no intention of getting mixed up with the German police. They'd probably be prejudiced against us from the start. On the other hand, in fairness to them, we've no right to remove anything from the scene of the crime. I'll leave the hair in Schneider's hand, just as we found it.' Biggles replaced the evidence, but retained one or two loose hairs, which he put in an envelope in his notecase.

'Aren't you even going to tell the police that a murder has been committed?' queried Ginger.

'No. It would do more harm than good. One thing would lead to another, and we should find ourselves faced with a choice of telling lies or answering embarrassing questions. Our reason for being in Germany would come out, and that wouldn't do at all. We'll leave the German police to work it out for themselves. They might resent our interference. I don't think there's much chance of their dropping on Preuss, and, in fact, I hope they don't, because, as I said just now, I'd rather he were free. Another aspect we mustn't overlook is this. If it became known in Germany that there was, in fact, an ex-Nazi gang, operating outlaw-fashion against the victorious nations, the head of the thing would be regarded, not as a criminal, but as a national hero. We must avoid that. It's happened before. Robin Hood, who made himself a thorn in the side of the Norman conquerors of Britain, provides a good example. To those who were trying to establish law and order he was a bandit; to the defeated Britons he was the cat's whisker. We'll behave as though we had never been here, although, of course, I shall report the incident to Raymond in due course. Later on, when we see more clearly how things are going, he may drop a hint to the German police.'

While Biggles had been speaking, Ginger's eyes, roving round the room, had come to rest on a small mirror over the mantelpiece. It may have been that a movement had attracted them. At all events, his glance was arrested by a movement; and he noticed that the door, which had been left open not more than a few inches, was ajar. And that was not all. Something—he could not at first make out what it was—was being projected into the room. It stopped, and at that instant he understood. With a shout of 'Look out!' he flung himself against Biggles with such violence that they both reeled across the room. Simultaneously there came a sharp hiss, and the mirror, with which Biggles had been in line, splintered into fragments that radiated from a central hole.

Ducking low Biggles made for the door, snatching out his pistol as he went. But he was too late. The door was snapped shut from the outside. A key grated in the lock. Keeping his body clear Biggles turned the handle and wrenched hard, but it was no use. The door remained closed.

'Of all the blithering idiots, I ought to be kicked from here to London,' he said bitingly. 'I noticed the key had gone, too. Thanks, laddie. You saved my bacon that time.'

He broke off and stood listening. For a little while there came a curious rustling sound from the other side of the door, then silence.

'He's gone,' breathed Ginger. 'For a moment, that silencer on the end of his pistol had me baffled. I spotted what it was just in time. We should have watched the door.'

Biggles shrugged. 'It's easy to blame yourself afterwards for being careless, but until you know just how far the enemy is prepared to go, it's hard to think of everything. Well, now we know. These people don't trouble to bluff, or threaten. They're killers, in the best American gangster style. While we were standing here talking the murderer was in that room opposite all the time. Or was he . . . I wonder? Schneider must have been dead by eight o'clock or he would have come to the hotel. It was half-past eight by the time we got here, which means that Schneider must have been dead for at least half an hour. Would the murderer hang about here for half an hour after he had committed the crime? I doubt it. Why should he? He couldn't have known we were coming here. On second thoughts I think it's more likely that Preuss, assuming he is the murderer, came along to the hotel to see what we were doing. Or he may have watched the house from the other side, to see if we came. Either way, there's no doubt that he saw us arrive, and crept up on us.'

'But what's his idea, locking us in?' asked Ginger wonderingly.

'I don't know,' answered Biggles. 'Maybe it was to keep us here with the corpse until the police came, and so saddle us with the murder—having failed to put a bullet through me.' As he spoke Biggles crossed to the window, and, lifting the blind at the corner, looked down.

Ginger joined him, and saw that the room overlooked the street. A man was just leaving the house, but what with the gloom, and the dark overcoat he was wearing, recognition was impossible. The man walked to a car that stood against the kerb a little higher up the street. He paused for a moment to look up; then he got in and drove away.

Ginger turned back into the room. As he did so his eyes fell on a line of smoke that was curling under the door. 'Hi! Look at this!' he cried. 'He's set the house on fire. That's why he's locked us in.'

'In that case we'd better see about getting out,' returned Biggles. 'It shouldn't be difficult—at least, not if he left the key in the lock. The woodwork in a cheap lodging-house like this is usually pretty flimsy. It'll mean making a noise, but that can't be prevented.'

This confident prediction turned out to be justified. Without much trouble Biggles was able to drive the leg of a chair through one of the thin panels of the door,

61

choosing the one nearest to the lock. This done, it was the work of a moment to put his hand through and turn the key. By this time a brisk fire, consisting mostly of old newspapers, was burning on the threshold; but there was no danger or difficulty in getting through. Biggles used the hearth-rug to smother the flames.

'No doubt it would suit Preuss if the whole building was gutted, because that would effectually obliterate everything,' he remarked, as he splashed water from the sink bowl over the smouldering embers until he was satisfied that the fire was really out. 'I think that'll do. With one thing and another this top floor should provide the German police with a pretty puzzle. One day we may explain what really happened. Come on.' Biggles set off down the stairs.

Apparently the residents of the establishment were accustomed to the noise, for none of them appeared, and the street was reached without an encounter.

'Now what?' asked Ginger.

'We may as well go back to the hotel,' decided Biggles, after a moment's reflection.

'What? You mean—you're going to let Preuss get away with this?'

Biggles shrugged. 'I don't see much point in following him to the aerodrome, assuming that's where he's gone. Even if we found him there, what could we do?'

'We could accuse him of killing Schneider.'

'A fat lot of good that would do. When all is said and done, Preuss isn't much more than a stooge.* My only interest in him is that he may lead us to the people

*Person doing the dirty work and, often, taking the blame while the real criminals escape.

we're really after. I doubt if we should find him at the aerodrome, anyway. He's probably in the air by now, in his ugly Swan. According to Schneider, when he makes these trips he's gone about twelve hours.' Biggles looked hard at Ginger. 'That gives me an idea. We might have a look round Preuss's office while he's away. If he's flying a compass course it's ten to one he made some calculations before he went—or at any rate, made some notes about his line of flight. Few pilots trust to memory. There's a wall map in his office, too. If he's in the habit of referring to it there may be some interesting pencil marks.'

'Preuss would lock his office before he went,' Ginger pointed out.

'Perhaps,' agreed Biggles. 'I'll tell you what we'll do. We'll go back to the hotel for a rest, and make a start before dawn—say, around four o'clock. I want to be on the aerodrome when Preuss comes back. You see, we've got to find these Renkell machines, and we shan't find them by cruising round the world haphazardly. The only man who knows where they are—as far as we know—is Preuss. He's working from here, so here we stay.'

As they went into the hotel the hall porter handed Biggles a cable. Biggles went over to one of the small tables, sat down and ripped the envelope. As he perused the flimsy sheet that it contained a ghost of a smile lifted the corners of his mouth.

'It's from Raymond,' he said softly. 'This is what he says. Max Grindler, sometimes known as The Pike, while serving a life sentence escaped from New York State Penitentiary two months ago, and hasn't been seen since. The Federal Bureau is still looking for him, but admits that it is baffled. Description: Age, forty-nine. Medium height and build. Black hair and grey eyes. Nose slightly bent. Little finger left hand missing.' Biggles folded the slip and put it in his pocket. 'Unless I'm wide of the mark, the American police are wasting their time,' he murmured. 'I'm not a betting man, but I'd risk a small wager that this particular fish is this side of the Atlantic. But let's try and get some sleep. I'll give you a shake about a quarter to four.'

Chapter 6
Getting Warmer

At a quarter to four Ginger was awakened by Biggles shaking his shoulder.

'On your feet,' ordered Biggles. 'We shall have to walk to the aerodrome.'

They arrived about half an hour later, and went first to the hangar that had been taken over by the R.A.F., where they found the Spur in charge of two airmen, in accordance with the arrangement made by Biggles with the wing commander. They had nothing to report. From them Biggles learned that an aircraft, presumably the Swan—they had heard it but not seen it—had taken off the previous evening about nine o'clock.

While they were talking at the hangar door Biggles more than once glanced curiously across the aerodrome in the direction of the Renkell works, whence came sounds of activity. An engine of some sort could be heard running.

'What goes on over there?' he asked the senior of the two airmen.

'We've often wondered that, sir,' was the answer.

'Often?' queried Biggles. 'Do you mean it's a regular thing?'

'Well, of course, we're not up here every night, so we couldn't say that,' replied the airman. 'But whenever I've been near the aerodrome at night someone has been hard at it in the Renkell machine shop.'

'I don't see any lights showing,' observed Biggles.

'I reckon they can't have taken their black-out blinds down yet,' suggested the airman.

'I see,' said Biggles slowly. 'All right, you fellows, stay here and look after the machine.'

'Very good, sir.'

Accompanied by Ginger, Biggles walked on towards the Renkell workshop—not directly, but keeping close against the buildings that lined the aerodrome boundary.

'What do you make of it?' asked Ginger.

'Queer business,' returned Biggles. 'The Renkell works are supposed to be doing nothing, yet here they are, running a night shift. Where's the money coming from to pay these chaps? And why the black-out? I'd say the two things go together. Something is going on in the works that outsiders are not intended to see, which means that it's fishy.'

'Making spare parts, perhaps, for the Renkell proto-types?' suggested Ginger.

'Either that, or they're building a new machine. Anyway, it rather upsets my plan. I expected to find the place quiet, closed down for the night. Still, there may be no one in Preuss's office. We shall have to find a way in without being seen.'

'That won't be by the door,' asserted Ginger. 'It opens straight into the workshop.'

Biggles went on, and after making a detour to locate the heap of old fabric that concealed the valve of the undeclared petrol store, he arrived at the workshop door. Cautiously, he tried the handle.

'Locked,' he said laconically. 'Let's go round to the

side and try the window of Preuss's office. I marked it down when we were in there.'

It turned out that this, too, was secured, but by climbing on Biggles' shoulders Ginger managed to make an entrance through another small window. He found himself in a lavatory. Leaving Biggles outside he went into the corridor and made his way along to the door that bore the manager's name, intending to open the window so that Biggles could enter. It was locked, but the door of the adjacent room, which turned out to be a small drawing-office, was open, so after closing the door behind him he crossed the room and unfastened the window, remarking, as Biggles joined him, 'Preuss's office is locked. This is the room next to it. There's a connecting door.'

This, too, was locked. With his penknife Biggles ascertained that the key had been left in the lock on the other side, but he was able to get it by the old trick of sliding a sheet of paper under the door and pushing the key out of the lock—again using the blade of his penknife—so that it fell on the paper. The paper was then withdrawn, bringing the key with it. Another moment and the door was open, and they had reached their objective—Preuss's office. After a glance at the window to make sure the blinds were drawn Biggles switched on the light. He paused to make a general survey of the room, and then walked to an overcoat that hung from a hook on the inside of the door.

'This is one of the things I expected to find,' he said quietly, as he felt in the side pockets. 'It isn't the sort of garment one would fly in, so I thought Preuss might leave it here!' He withdrew his hand and held it out for Ginger to see. It was moist, and stained—red. 'That settles any doubt as to who killed Schneider,' he resumed. 'Preuss got rid of the weapon, but until he did he carried it in his pocket. We'll remember this coat if ever we need evidence.'

A quick examination of the room yielded only one more item of interest. In a small toilet attached to the office Ginger found a shaving kit that had recently been used. Judging from the state in which it had been left the user had been in a hurry. Biggles recovered a number of long fair hairs from the grid at the top of the waste pipe.

'A man doesn't shave his head,' he observed. 'It looks as if Preuss has taken off his moustache.'

'That won't be much of a disguise,' sneered Ginger.

'I don't think that was the idea,' returned Biggles. 'Remember the tuft of hair in Schneider's hand? We assumed it was torn from Preuss's head, but in view of this I'd say it came from his moustache. Rather than walk about with lopsided whiskers Preuss has made a clean job by taking the lot off—at least, that's how it looks to me.'

A close scrutiny of the wall map did not reveal the pencil marks Biggles hoped to find. Nor was there anything of interest in, or on, the desk, which was furnished with the usual office equipment. The only unusual object—not unusual, perhaps, considering the proximity of the drawing-office—was a pair of dividers which lay on the blotting-pad with legs wide apart. Ginger would have picked them up, but Biggles stopped him.

'Just a minute,' he said. 'We may have something here. I've used a pair of dividers a good many times to plot a course—so have you. Preuss probably used these for the same purpose. The trouble about using dividers is that one is apt to prick the map, particularly at one's base, which is always the central point—for which reason maps captured from airmen are highly esteemed by the Intelligence Branch. If the distance between the points of this instrument are in relation to the scale of the map, Preuss has gone a long way—not less than a thousand miles, for a guess. Let's try our luck.'

Crossing to the map he lifted it from its nail, and, standing behind it, held it up against the electric light globe. 'Ah,' he breathed. 'Now we're getting somewhere. Come and look at this.'

Joining him, Ginger saw a number of tiny points of light where the map had been punctured, most of them grouped closely around one that was larger than the rest. At some distance lower on the map there was a single isolated puncture.

'The large hole will, of course, be Augsburg,' said Biggles. 'It's larger than the rest because whatever journey is intended it is always used. Those surrounding it are so close that they must be other aerodromes in Germany. Bear in mind that over a period of time several people have probably used this map. The hole that interests me is this little fellow all by itself, way down south.' Biggles applied the dividers, and clicked his tongue triumphantly when the points of the instrument precisely covered the gap between it and Augsburg.

The back of the map was, of course, plain; there was nothing to indicate the geographical position of the localities marked. But these were soon ascertained. Biggles ordered Ginger to go round to the front of the map and name the places where a point of the dividers appeared.

'That should be Augsburg,' he averred, making his first point.

'Quite right,' confirmed Ginger.

'What about this one?' Biggles inserted the point in the lower puncture.

'You're in Africa—North Africa,' answered Ginger in a tense voice.

'North Africa is a big place—kindly be a little more precise,' invited Biggles.

'Tripolitania—close to Tripoli,' said Ginger. 'By gosh! I've got it. It's Castel Benito aerodrome.'

'We're getting warm,' declared Biggles. 'I'm not interested in the other places—they're all more or less local. I don't think the map will tell us any more.' He re-hung it on the wall.

'You think Castel Benito is the base from which the gang is operating?' inquired Ginger eagerly.

Biggles shook his head. 'No. They may use it—in fact, that seems certain. But so do other people use it. I should say it's more likely that Castel Benito is the jumping-off place for the real hide-out. No matter, we're on the track.'

'How about running down to Castel Benito on the chance of finding Preuss there?' suggested Ginger.

'If he follows his usual procedure he will already be on his way back,' Biggles pointed out. 'Apart from that, we can't leave here until we get the message from Algy. We'll wait for Preuss to come in—we may learn something. We could always run down to Tripoli later on. But let's get out of this while the going's good.'

They left the office as they had entered, locking the

door behind them and leaving the key in the lock. As they dropped through the window to the tarmac the hum of the power plant in the workshop died away. Dawn was just breaking.

Biggles glanced at his watch. 'Six o'clock,' he observed. 'The men are knocking off work.'

'Aren't you going to try to find out what they are doing?' asked Ginger.

'I don't care much what they're doing,' answered Biggles. 'The knowledge wouldn't help us. These fellows are only accessories; they may not even know what the gang is doing. Neither do we, for certain, if it comes to that. Let's go over to the hangar and get out of sight.'

'If we've got to search the whole of Tripolitania looking for the Renkells we've got a big job in front of us,' remarked Ginger, as they walked on.

'I'm hoping it won't come to that,' replied Biggles. 'When we know where Baumer and Scaroni served during the North African campaigns I fancy we shall be on the right track. I'll tell you what. There's no need for both of us to stay here on the aerodrome. You stick around and watch for the Swan to come back. Make a note of what Preuss does and try to get a dekko* at the machine. If it's been in the desert there should be sand stuck on the oil stains, for instance. I'll go down to the hotel and wait for the messages. If I see Howath I'll ask him to use his private wire to get a signal through to Alexandria asking Algy and Bertie to stay there pending further instructions. There's no point in their coming all the way back. If I miss

*Slang: look.

71

Howath, you can ask him to send the signal when he comes in. I also want to get in touch with the Yard, to see if they've discovered anything about Scaroni. I'll join you later. Call me on the telephone if Preuss comes back.' Biggles departed.

It was nine-thirty when he returned to the aerodrome, and he raised his eyebrows in surprise when Ginger told him that the Swan had not shown up.

'In that case I'll take over while you slip down to the hotel for breakfast,' suggested Biggles. 'When you're through, you may as well pay the bill and check out.'

'Then you're leaving?'

'Yes.'

'What about the messages?'

'I've got them. Algy found the wheel marks on the sand about twenty miles north of Bahrain. He landed and measured the track. It was four metres, which confirms, definitely, that the Renkell prototypes are the machines being used by the crooks. I never had much doubt about it, but now we have concrete evidence. The chance of another machine with that wheel track— even if one exists—landing on the shore of the Persian Gulf, is so remote that we needn't consider it. I saw Howath, and got him to send a signal to Alex to hold the Mosquito there until we get in touch. Another interesting item of news I got from the Yard is, Scaroni was an officer in the regular Italian Air Force. Nearly all his service was in North Africa. He was supply and transport officer attached to Escadrille Thirty-three, which fought in Abyssinia, and was later stationed at Benghazi, Castel Benito, and El Zufra.'

'Where the deuce is El Zufra?'

'I looked it up. It's an oasis right down in the Libyan

72

desert. The Italians must have used it during the fighting there. The most interesting thing about that is, if Scaroni was in charge of transport and supplies, he would have the handling of the petrol. Maybe he alone knows where a lot of it was hidden when the Italians were pushed out of their African Empire.* Anyway, it's a million pounds to a brass farthing that it is from such a dump that the Renkell machines are getting their oil and petrol. The thing begins to fit together. Baumer had the machines. Scaroni had the petrol. Gontermann, who is wanted by the British authorities anyway, has knowledge and experience of the jewel trade, and crook methods of disposing of gems. Preuss, in the Swan, runs a communication machine between the gang and civilisation, in case anything is urgently needed. Just how Renkell fits in we have yet to find out—unless he's a sort of general mechanic.'

'What about this alleged American?' queried Ginger.

'That's a puzzler,' confessed Biggles. 'As I see it, one of two things happened. Either Gontermann, thinking he could use him, got him out of jail, or else Grindler— if it is Grindler—got out on his own account and came over here gunning for Gontermann—the man who had squealed on him. Having caught up with him he learned about the new racket; so instead of bumping Gontermann off, and returning to the States, broke, and a hunted man into the bargain, he joined the gang, which gave him a chance of keeping clear of the police and making a packet of money at the same time. By

---

*Italy conquered Ethiopia, then called Abyssinia, in 1935–6 and created an African Empire, but were defeated in 1941 by British and Abyssinian forces.

the way, I've told the Yard that we shall be leaving here shortly.'

'Did the B.B.C. pick up anything on the air?'

'No—not so far. They're still listening.'

'Have you decided definitely to go to Africa?'

'Yes. I want to see Preuss land, first, though.'

'Okay,' agreed Ginger. 'I'll slip down for some breakfast and bring the kit along.' He went off.

When he returned an hour later Biggles was still sitting in the hangar. He looked perplexed.

'Isn't Preuss back *yet*?' cried Ginger.

'Not a sign of him,' answered Biggles. 'Apparently, either something has happened to keep him at Castel Benito, or wherever he's gone, or else he's had a forced landing.'

'Perhaps he isn't coming back. Maybe he's got the wind up, and bolted?' offered Ginger.

'That didn't occur to me,' admitted Biggles. 'I must admit it's a possibility, although I can't think it's likely. I made a mistake in assuming that he was coming straight back because he always has done so in the past. It's time I knew that it doesn't do to take anything for granted. His non-return certainly makes a difference. For one thing, it means that unless he's also going to break his rule about daylight flying he won't start back until this evening, in which case we could get to North Africa before he leaves. We'll give him a little longer. If he isn't back by noon we'll make a fast run down to Castel Benito in the hope of catching him there.'

'With what particular object?'

'It would confirm that Castel Benito is being used by the gang.'

74

'He'll see us, and tip off the gang not to use the aerodrome any more.'

'What of it? They can't have many landing-grounds available, and by scotching them off we shall cramp their style.'

When noon came, and still Preuss did not show up, Biggles climbed into his seat, took off, and headed south.

The Spur covered the twelve hundred miles between Augsburg and Tripoli at cruising speed in a trifle over four hours, arriving in sight of the hot, dusty aerodrome, shortly after four o'clock. While they were still some distance away Ginger noted two aircraft on the ground. Both were painted yellow. One was the Swan. It was just taking off. He shouted, but Biggles had also seen it, and swerved to the west, into the glare of the sinking sun, to avoid being seen. The Swan held on a straight course due north.

'He took off in daylight after all!' cried Ginger.

'It will be dusk by the time he reaches the far side of the Mediterranean,' Biggles pointed out.

Ginger turned to look at the second machine, and saw that it was streaking across the aerodrome towards the south-east. He uttered a cry of amazement, for although he had never seen the machine before he knew from its unorthodox lines that it was the Renkell transport.

'By gosh! We've got it!' he cried.

'Got what?' asked Biggles evenly.

'The Renkell! Aren't you going to follow it?'

'Look at the petrol gauge,' invited Biggles.

Ginger looked, and saw with dismay that they were down to the last few gallons. He groaned.

'I don't mind taking risks,' went on Biggles, 'but I draw the line at starting off across the Libyan desert with an empty tank.'

'We can fill up at the aerodrome.'

'By the time I've got this aircraft on the ground, and refuelled, the Renkell will be a hundred miles away,' answered Biggles dryly.

'Then what are we going to do?' asked Ginger, in a disappointed voice.

'We'll get some juice in the tank for a start,' replied Biggles, as he took the Spur down and landed, finishing his run near the control building, adding another little cloud of dust to those that had been thrown up by the departing machines.

As they climbed out, an unshaven man in a faded, untidy Italian uniform, came to meet them. Apart from him the aerodrome was deserted. The buildings still showed marks of the war.

'Are you in charge here?' asked Biggles in English.

'I am da manager,' was the curt reply, in the same language.

'I need some petrol,' announced Biggles.

'No petrol.'

Biggles started. 'What! What about those two machines that just took off? You filled them up with petrol didn't you?'

'*Si, signor,** but they had special carnets,' was the suave reply.

'Is that so?' murmured Biggles frostily, looking hard

---

*Italian: Yes, Sir.

at the man. 'Now you listen to me, *amico*,* I've got a special carnet, too, so trot out your petrol, *presto*.**'

The Italian affected a look of distress. 'But the *meccanos*** — they are resting.'

Biggles tapped him gently on the chest. '*Signor*,' he said softly, 'I'm on British Government business. If my machine isn't refuelled by the time I've had a cup of coffee — say, twenty minutes — I shall make a report that there is an obstructionist at Castel Benito. If I do that you can start looking for a new job. Now, do I get the petrol?'

'*Si, signor*,' muttered the Italian.

'I shall keep an eye on you through the window,' cautioned Biggles, and walked on towards a door conspicuously marked, *Ristorante*.

'From that fellow's attitude I should say he's in the racket,' remarked Ginger.

'Of course he is,' agreed Biggles. 'Or at any rate, he's on the pay-roll. There's no other reason why he should deny us the petrol. No doubt he would have produced some eventually, but he had no intention of doing so until these crook machines were well on their way. The Renkell, I imagine, has departed for its base, and from the line it took that might be El Zufra. The oasis lies south-east from here. The two machines met on this aerodrome. Was that, I wonder, a previous arrangement, or did Preuss dash down to warn the gang that inquiries were being made at Augsburg?'

---

*Italian: Friend.
**Italian: Quick.
***Italian: Mechanics.

'Either way, no doubt he's tipped them off,' asserted Ginger.

'He's bound to have done that,' agreed Biggles. 'How much he has told them depends on how much he himself knows about us. One thing is certain. We're a lot nearer to the headquarters of the gang than we were at Augsburg. I don't suppose there will be anybody in here, so we'll talk things over.'

Biggles pushed open the door of the restaurant and went in.

On this occasion he was wrong. A man, a youngish, dark-skinned man, dressed in slovenly tropical kit, was sitting at a small table drinking coffee. A peculiar feeling came over Ginger that he had seen him before, but he could not remember where. For a moment he groped in the mist of uncertainty; then, in a flash, he knew. He had seen the man, but not in life. He had seen his photograph, and he had seen it too recently for there to be any mistake. It was the Italian ex-officer whose portrait Biggles had found in Preuss's office—Carlos Scaroni.

Ginger glanced at Biggles, knowing that he, too, must have recognised him. But Biggles' face, as he pulled out a chair at another table and sat down, was expressionless. However, after a moment or two his eyes met Ginger's. He winked.

'That's something I *didn't* expect,' he murmured.

Scaroni took not the slightest notice of them, which puzzled Ginger not a little, because even though the Italian had never seen them before, he must have watched the machine land; and if Preuss had mentioned them he would certainly have described the aircraft that had landed at Augsburg, particularly an outstanding aircraft like the Spur. At least, so thought Ginger.

His cogitations were interrupted when an inner door was opened and a second man appeared. He was immaculately, if somewhat loudly, dressed in ultra-smart European clothes. Ginger was astonished when he joined the Italian, for they were an ill-matched pair. The table, he now noticed, was laid for two. Then the newcomer spoke to his companion.

'Say, why don't you run your ships on time, like we do in the States?' he drawled irritably.

Ginger stiffened when Biggles addressed the American—it was so unexpected.

'Excuse me,' said Biggles, 'but I couldn't help overhearing your remark. Do I understand that a regular service runs through here?'

'Sure,' was the easy reply. 'The dagoes* have got a line running from Rome to Alex, via Tripoli and Benghazi. We're waiting for it, but like everything else in this goldarned country, it's late.'

'Thanks,' acknowledged Biggles.

At this point the Italian said something to his companion in a voice so low that Ginger did not catch the words. Whatever it was, it altered the expression on the American's face. His right hand moved slowly inside his coat towards his left armpit, and his eyes, pale and cold like those of a fish, came round to rest on Biggles's face.

'You figgerin' on staying in these parts, mister?' he asked, in a thin, dry voice.

*Offensive slang term for the Latin races – Spanish, Italian and South Americans.

'Maybe,' answered Biggles noncommittally.

'I wouldn't,' drawled the American.

'Why not?' inquired Biggles.

'It's bad country—bad for the health,' was the cold reply.

Ginger was conscious of a dryness in the mouth. He heard the conversation, as it were, from a distance. For his eyes were on the American's left hand. The little finger was missing.

Chapter 7
Gloves Off

To Ginger, certain things were now clear. The American was Grindler. Of that there was no doubt. The description tallied. And Grindler knew who they were. He had not known when he returned to the room, but Scaroni had known. Naturally, he being a pilot, would recognise the aircraft, a description of which had evidently been furnished by Preuss. To Grindler, a layman, one aircraft was much as another, but Scaroni had lost no time in making him acquainted with the true state of affairs. There was no need to wonder what Grindler carried under his left arm, that he should so automatically reach for it.

When the shock of this disconcerting discovery had passed, and Ginger's nerves returned more or less to normal, Biggles was ordering coffee from a slatternly Italian waitress. Except for a ghost of a smile Biggles's expression was unchanged; but as soon as the waitress had gone he said softly, 'Okay, I've seen it. We're on thin ice, but take it easy.'

Grindler and Scaroni were also engaged in low and earnest conversation. Grindler—his hand was still under his jacket—appeared to be emphatic about something. The Italian looked nervous.

'I fancy Grindler is advocating a little gun-play, to settle any further argument,' murmured Biggles.

'What if he has his way?'

Biggles shrugged. 'I'm afraid there would be casualties. In America a gangster doesn't climb to the top of the tree unless he's pretty snappy with a gun. It only needs a spark to set things alight.'

'That's comforting,' grunted Ginger sarcastically.

At this juncture Scaroni left the room abruptly. Through the window Ginger could see him in serious conversation with the airport manager. The gangster lolled in his chair, picking his teeth nonchalantly with a match-stalk; but his eyes never left Biggles.

The waitress brought the coffee. She, too, was obviously nervous. Then Scaroni, after a glance at the sky, hurried back to the restaurant. The drone of an aircraft became audible. The airport manager came in and presented Biggles with a bill for the petrol, which he paid in English money rather than display his official carnet.

The plane, a Caproni bomber adapted for commercial use, landed, and this broke the tension. Scaroni and Grindler picked up their luggage—two small suitcases—and walked to the door, where the American turned.

'Remember what I said about your health,' he said, and followed the Italian to the Caproni. No passengers alighted, so they went straight on board. The aircraft took off again, heading east.

Ginger drew a deep breath. 'Phew! When we barged in here we bit off plenty,' he asserted. 'I didn't like that atmosphere at all. What's the programme? Not much use staying here, is it?'

'No use at all,' returned Biggles. 'What in thunder are Scaroni and Grindler up to, going to Egypt in a civil plane? That's a poser. We may as well push along that way ourselves. We'll keep an eye on them, and make contact with Algy and Bertie.'

'It looks to me as if we've sort of stirred things up,' opined Ginger. 'As I see it, Preuss came here to meet the gang. Baumer must have been flying the Renkell. Scaroni obviously recognised our machine, which means that Preuss must have told him about our arrival at Augsburg. As the Swan and the Renkell were here together, Baumer, as well as Scaroni, must have heard what Preuss had to say. Scaroni put Grindler wise when he came in. In short, the whole bunch now knows about us. What puzzles me is, why did the Renkell bring Scaroni and Grindler here, when it might as well have taken them to Egypt—presumably to Alexandria.'

'The probable answer to that is, it wouldn't do to have the Renkell seen flying over Egypt, where it could hardly fail to attract attention. Scaroni and Grindler prefer to arrive at Alex in a manner less conspicuous. As far as the police are concerned they are two ordinary, well-behaved passengers. We know they're crooks, but knowing isn't enough; we've got to prove it, and that's something we can't do—yet. They made this the rendezvous because the manager here is on their pay-roll. He made that clear by the way he argued about petrol until the two machines were well on their way. Well, we shan't find out what Scaroni and Grindler are up to in Alex by sitting here. Let's push on. We shall be there long before they are.'

They paid the bill for the coffee, went out to the Spur, and took off. Biggles headed west.

'Here, you're going the wrong way!' cried Ginger.

'For the moment,' replied Biggles. 'I don't want that

airport manager sending word along to Scaroni and Grindler that we're following them.'

Biggles edged towards the sea, but as soon as the landing-ground had dropped below the horizon he swung round and raced east in the track of the Caproni. Flying high, they passed Benghazi at sunset, giving the aerodrome a wide berth in order not to be seen should the Caproni be there. They went on and landed at Alexandria in the light of the brilliant Egyptian moon. Having checked in and parked the machine they made their way to the aerodrome hotel, where they found Algy and Bertie, looking extremely bored, waiting for a message.

Without delay Biggles gave them a concise résumé of events.

'I've got a job for you two,' he concluded. 'In a few minutes the Caproni will land. This isn't the time to start a rumpus, so Ginger and I will keep out of the way; but neither Scaroni nor Grindler knows you, so you should be able to keep an eye on them without arousing suspicion. I want to know what they do. You've taken rooms here, I suppose?'

'Of course,' confirmed Algy.

'All right. Ginger and I will do the same. Let us know what happens. You'll find us in our rooms. I've done enough flying for one day, so I shan't move unless something startling occurs. This tearing round the world is hard work.' Crossing to the office, finding that there were no single rooms available, he booked a double room for Ginger and himself.

Half an hour later they were lying on their beds discussing the situation, when Bertie entered hurriedly.

'You're soon back,' remarked Biggles, looking surprised.

'Back? We haven't been anywhere, old boy,' declared Bertie. 'No need. Scaroni and Grindler are staying right here in the hotel—and when I say staying I mean staying. They're in their rooms now. We heard them giving orders that they were not to be disturbed. They're to be called at eight-thirty in the morning, to catch the nine o'clock plane.'

Biggles sat up. 'Catch what plane?'

Bertie rubbed his eyeglass briskly. 'I know it sounds silly, and all that, but they've booked passages to London.'

'The deuce they have!' ejaculated Biggles. 'By what line?'

'Our own—British Overseas Airways, or whatever they call it now. They travel in the *Calpurnia*, the Empire flying-boat* that leaves at nine.'

Biggles thrust his hands into his pockets. 'That beats cock-fighting,' he declared. 'What on earth can they be going to do in London? I should have made a thousand guesses as to where they were bound for—and been wrong every time. Bertie, you and Algy will have to go with them. Slip down and book two seats.'

'I say, what fun,' murmured Bertie, and departed.

In five minutes he was back. Algy came with him. 'Nothing doing,' he informed them. 'The boat's full. Every seat has been booked.'

Biggles lit a cigarette. 'This has got me completely

---

*Four engined flying boats, made by Short Brothers, were designed to carry mail & passengers to all parts of the British Empire. They were in use 1936–1947.

cheesed,' he confessed. 'All right. There's only one thing to do. You'll have to follow them right through to London in the Mosquito. Find Raymond, and tell him I want these two men shadowed. Cable me any news. Ginger and I will hang on here, in case they come back.'

'Okay,' agreed Algy.

'You'd better go and get some sleep,' advised Biggles. 'Tell the office we all want calling at eight o'clock sharp. We'll have breakfast in our rooms.'

Biggles had a restless night, and he was up, dressed, at eight o'clock, when breakfast was brought in. Shortly afterwards Algy and Bertie arrived.

'The more I think of this development the less I like it,' averred Biggles, walking about with his coffee in his hand. 'I swear there's a trick in it somewhere, but I'm dashed if I can see it.'

'Is this trip to London a red herring, to lure us off the scent?' suggested Algy.

'I've considered that, but I don't see how it can be,' answered Biggles. 'This trip must have been planned before we arrived on the scene. At any rate, Scaroni and Grindler had arranged to come to Alex. They booked to London the moment they got here, so that must have been part of the plan. No, I'm convinced that this was all fixed up some time ago. Scaroni and Grindler don't know we're here, so they're going on with their scheme—whatever that may be. We'll come down with you and watch the machine out, to make sure they actually travel in it. If they do, you Algy, and Bertie, can waffle along to England. You needn't hurry. In the Mosquito you'll be there before they are.'

'Right you are,' agreed Algy.

At a few minutes to nine, from a safe distance, they watched Scaroni and Grindler join the *Calpurnia* and take their places. At nine-five the flying-boat had still not taken off, and there appeared to be a consultation between the officials.

'What's the argument about, I wonder?' murmured Ginger.

'Some of the passengers haven't turned up,' answered Biggles. 'I've seen only six people get into that machine, not counting the crew. Ah! It looks as if they've decided to go without them,' he concluded, as the *Calpurnia* was cast off.

The engines came to life; the big aircraft taxied majestically into position for its take-off, and in a few minutes was in the air, heading west.

'Well, they're on board, that's certain, so we may as well be getting along, too,' suggested Algy, and Biggles agreed.

'I still don't understand it,' Biggles told Ginger, some little while later, after the Mosquito had taken off. 'Even if a few of the passengers had been on board before we arrived, that flying-boat took off with half its seats empty. Yet when we tried to book we were told that every seat had been taken. It's not an unusual thing for one, or perhaps two passengers, to cancel, but that a dozen should do so strikes me as being too odd to be reasonable. I'm going to have a word with the traffic manager. Come on.'

In a few minutes they were in the traffic manager's office. Biggles showed his credentials.

'What can I do for you?' queried the official.

'Last night we were told that the nine o'clock plane

for London had been booked to capacity,' asserted Biggles. 'It took off half empty. What went wrong?'

The traffic manager looked nonplussed. 'I don't know,' he admitted. 'I've never seen anything like it. Occasionally we get a cancellation, but these bookings didn't trouble to cancel. The passengers just didn't turn up, so they won't get a refund on their tickets. In the end we had to go without them. We can't hold up the air mail.'

A peculiar expression came over Biggles's face. 'Do you mean you carry the London mail?' he asked.

'Yes.'

'Was there anything particularly valuable in it?'

'Not as far as I know,' answered the official. 'There was the usual bag of registered letters, of course. Why do you ask?'

'Because,' replied Biggles, 'there happens to be an expert jewel thief among the passengers. He has a partner with him, too.'

The manager sprang to his feet in agitation. 'Good God! You don't tell me such a thing!'

'That's what I am telling you,' rapped out Biggles. 'What's wrong?'

The colour had drained from the official's face. 'I must get to the signals-room and get in touch with the radio operator at once,' he said in a voice hoarse with alarm. He started for the door.

'Just a minute,' snapped Biggles. 'Why the sudden anxiety?'

'Because,' answered the traffic manager, 'there are jewels in that aircraft worth a king's ransom. It's the regalia of the Rajah of Mysalore. His Highness is already in London for the Empire Conference. He offered to lend his regalia to some exhibition in aid of the Red Cross.'

'How were these jewels being carried?' asked Biggles, in a brittle voice.

'By special courier. The little man in the dark over-coat was carrying them in an attaché-case. Look, out of my way, I must radio—'

'I'm afraid anything you can do will be too late,' broke in Biggles. 'I see the scheme, now. Those seats were never intended to be occupied. They were booked by the crooks to keep the machine empty. We'll do what we can. The best thing you can do is to try to get in touch with that Mosquito that followed the *Calpurnia* out. It's flown by one of my men. Tell him to try to pick up the *Calpurnia* and keep it in sight. Come on, Ginger.'

Biggles ran to the hangar and ordered the Spur out. He was still panting when he climbed into his seat, and sent the machine roaring into the air.

'I'm losing my grip,' he told Ginger furiously. 'I should have suspected something of the sort. It was all so simple.'

'But I don't see what the crooks can do,' demurred Ginger. 'Suppose they get the attaché-case? How can they get away with it? The Renkell isn't an amphibian. It can't land on the water to pick them up.'

'You haven't by any chance forgotten that Scaroni is a pilot?' grated Biggles. 'Once Grindler has disposed of the crew, Scaroni can take the *Calpurnia* anywhere. I'm going to gamble that he'll head for the beach on the African side in order to make contact with the Renkell at some pre-arranged spot. We'll chance it, and follow the coast. We couldn't do anything over the sea, even if we picked up the *Calpurnia*.'

For nearly an hour, flying on full throttle, Biggles followed the flat sandy beach of the North African coast. On the right hand lay the Mediterranean, an expanse of colour representing every shade of blue and green, according to the depth of the water. To the left, the barren earth, still littered with the debris of war, rolled back until it merged into the haze of the far horizon. The haze was unusual, but the weather had deteriorated somewhat; banks of fleecy cloud were drifting up from the west. The shattered remains of Mersa Matruh, Sidi Barrani, and Sollum*, villages of poignant memory, flashed past below, and Biggles had just remarked that Tobruk came next when he moved suddenly, leaning forward in his seat.

'There they are!' he exclaimed. 'Both machines are on the beach. I'm afraid we're going to be just too late.'

Looking ahead, Ginger saw the great flying-boat on its side in shallow water. It appeared to have been driven ashore at high speed regardless of damage. A short distance away, on the smooth, dry sand, just beyond the reach of the foam that made a lacy pattern on the beach, stood the Renkell transport, its idling airscrews flashing in the sparkling atmosphere. Even as Ginger watched he saw two men jump from the flying-boat and run towards the Renkell. One carried a small, black attaché-case. He threw a glance at the

*Battlefields in the fight against the Italians during 1940 and later the Germans during 1941–2.

approaching aircraft and then raced on, and Ginger knew they had been seen.

In the Middle East distance is deceptive, and the Spur was still a mile away when the Renkell took off. The instant its wheels were clear of the ground, it banked steeply and sped away towards the south, racing low over the wilderness.

'We've got the height; we ought to be able to catch him,' said Biggles tersely.

'You'll use your guns?' queried Ginger.

'You bet I will, if he won't go down,' answered Biggles. 'This is a better chance than I dared to hope for—to catch them red-handed, with the swag on them.' His thumb covered the firing button on the control column. 'Keep your eyes on the sky,' he ordered. 'The other Renkell, the Wolf, may be prowling about in those clouds.'

The words had hardly died on his lips, and Ginger had started to turn, to man the gun-turret, when above the roar of the engines came the harsh grunting of machine-guns. In a flash Biggles had dragged the control column back into his right thigh, sending the Spur up in a wild zoom; but quick though he had been, several bullets struck the machine. Ginger felt the vibration of their impact. As he grabbed for his guns the Wolf tore past, pulling up at the bottom of its dive, so close that Ginger flinched, thinking they had collided. He heard Biggles's guns snarling, and then a douche of ice-cold spirit on his legs wrung from him a cry of dismay. He clawed his way to Biggles. It was necessary to claw, literally, for not for an instant was the Spur on even keel.

'He got us!' he yelled. 'The tank's holed. There's

petrol all over the place. Hold your fire, or we shall go up in a sheet of flame.*' He dropped into his seat, and through the windscreen saw the Wolf vanishing into the cloud. The transport had already disappeared.

Biggles cut his engines and turned back towards the beach. His face was pale with anger and chagrin.

'I'm game to go on if you are,' offered Ginger.

'There's no sense in committing suicide,' rasped Biggles. 'I should have guessed that the Wolf would act as escort to the transport. I took a look round, but it must have been in those infernal clouds. He got the first crack at us. Baumer knows his job all right.' Biggles glided down towards the area of beach off which the flying-boat lay.

'But just a minute!' exclaimed Ginger. 'This means they've got three pilots. Scaroni was in the *Calpurnia*. Baumer could have flown the transport or the Wolf, but not both.'

'That's pretty obvious,' agreed Biggles, as he went on down and landed on the sand.

Another machine, flying high, was just coming in from the sea. It was the Mosquito.

*In air combat, petrol vapour can easily be ignited by the flashes from the muzzles of the guns.

Chapter 8
Biggles Follows On

On the ground, all was tragedy and disaster, and the hard, frosty look that Ginger knew so well, came into Biggles's eyes.

In the wrecked flying-boat both the first and second pilots lay dead, shot through the head. The wireless operator lay asprawl his instrument. He, too, was dead. The courier to whom the jewels had been entrusted was just expiring. An automatic close by his hand suggested that he would have put up a fight had he been given the opportunity. One of the passengers, who turned out to be an officer going home on leave from India, sprawled in a seat, deathly pale, a shattered arm dangling horribly. The steward and the four other passengers—two elderly tourists with their wives, one British and one American—had made their way to the beach, where they stood talking. They were shaken, but unhurt. After giving first aid to the wounded officer it was from one of these that Biggles presently got the story, a story that caused his lips to compress in a thin hard line.

By this time the Mosquito had landed. In a few words Biggles explained what had happened. Algy, in turn, revealed that they had picked up the radio message sent out by the traffic manager at Alexandria. They had found the *Calpurnia* off its course, heading south, but had lost it in the cloud. By following its last known course, southward, they had arrived in sight of the coast, and were following it back to Alexandria when they spotted the flying-boat grounded in the surf.

The story of events in the *Calpurnia*, told by the passenger, were much as Biggles expected.

The thing began, he said, when the wireless operator came into the cabin, and going to the courier whispered something in his ear. (From this Ginger realised that the operator must have picked up the alarm signal sent out by Alexandria. He had warned the courier of his danger, which was all he could do.) The wireless operator—went on the passenger—had returned to his compartment. Two men then got up and walked to the forward bulkhead, to the door that gave access to the cockpit. Through this they disappeared, although a notice proclaimed that entry was prohibited. A moment later there came the sound of a shot. The passenger explained that he was not sure of this at the time; he thought it might be one of the engines misfiring. Apparently this was the shot that killed the wireless operator. Then came two more shots. At the same time the flying-boat swerved. This, the listeners realised, must have been the moment when the pilots were murdered in cold blood. Up to this time none of the passengers had reason to suspect that anything serious was afoot. The first indication of that came when one of the two men reappeared, an automatic in his hand. Standing in the doorway he covered the passengers and informed them that he would shoot the first person who moved. This man, asserted the passenger, spoke with an American accent. In spite of this threat the courier had jumped to his feet and pulled out a pistol. The gunman promptly shot him, unnecessarily firing a second shot into him after he was on the floor; whereupon another passenger—the officer—had flung a book at the murderer and then tried to close with him. But this, while brave, was foolish, and all he succeeded in getting was a bullet through the arm that shattered the bone. The other passengers, helpless, sat still, for which they were hardly to be blamed. Thus matters had remained for some time. The course of the aircraft had been altered from west to south. Later, with the gunman still keeping the passengers covered, the *Calpurnia* had been landed, and taxied to the beach where another machine was waiting. The gunman, who had already picked up the courier's attaché-case, with his companion, then changed machines and flew off. That was all.

'I see,' said Biggles quietly, when this grim recital was finished. 'For your information—but please keep this to yourselves for the time being—the little man who was shot was carrying a parcel of very valuable jewels. His assailants were jewel thieves.'

'Even so, there was no need for them to commit murder,' muttered one of the women passengers.

'To the people behind this affair murder is nothing new,' returned Biggles. 'But we mustn't stand talking here any longer. I have one serviceable aircraft, and although I need it badly myself I shall have to use it to get the wounded officer back to Alexandria. He is in urgent need of medical attention. Unfortunately, the machine will only carry one passenger, so the rest of you will have to wait until a relief plane arrives.' Biggles turned to Algy. 'I had better stay here,' he went on. 'You take the Mosquito and fly this officer to Alex. Explain what has happened, and ask for a relief plane to be sent to pick up the passengers. It had better bring a working party along; there may be a chance to do some salvage work on the *Calpurnia*. They'd better bring some petrol, too. Get back here as quickly as you can.' Biggles took Algy out of earshot of the passengers. 'You might ask the authorities to keep the story out of the Press as long as possible. In any case, in no circumstances do we want our names mentioned in connection with the affair. That's important.'

'Good enough,' agreed Algy, and in a few minutes was in the air, with the wounded officer as passenger, heading east.

After that there was nothing the others could do but wait. The steward waded out to the *Calpurnia*, and managed to produce a substantial lunch, which in the ordinary way would have been served on the machine.

The sun was well past its zenith when Algy returned, bringing the traffic manager with him. Biggles had to take him into his confidence, and explanations occupied some time. A relief plane, said the official, was on the way. It was bringing mechanics and petrol.

'I'd be obliged if you'd let your men repair the Spur before they start on the *Calpurnia*,' requested Biggles. 'I shall want to use it.'

To this the manager agreed.

'What are you going to do?' Algy asked Biggles.

'I'm going to make a reconnaissance while the trail is still warm,' answered Biggles. 'There's nothing else we can do that I can see. I'll take the Mosquito and have a look at this place El Zufra. The oasis is due south from here, and the Renkell's headed in that direction. Ginger can come with me. As soon as the Spur is serviceable, fill up with petrol and follow on. I doubt

96

if that'll be this side of nightfall, though. If you can't get away before sunset you'd better wait for dawn, rather than risk missing the oasis in the dark. This is assuming that we're not back by then. Of course, if there's nothing at Zufra we shall come straight back and contact you here.'

Bertie broke in. 'I say, old boy, what are you going to do if you find the Renkells at this beastly place Zufra?'

'I shall endeavour to shoot them up, to ensure that they stay there,' answered Biggles grimly. 'Come on, Ginger, let's get cracking.'

By this time it was nearly five o'clock, with the sun sinking like an enormous toy balloon towards the western horizon.

Biggles walked over to the Mosquito, collecting his map from the damaged Spur on the way. In the cockpit, with Ginger sitting on his left, he opened the map and put a finger on a name printed in tiny italics, conspicuous only because it occurred on the vast and otherwise blank area of the Libyan desert.

'That's Oasis El Zufra, our objective,' he said. 'Don't ask me what there is there because I don't know. I expect it's much the same as any other Libyan oasis— a few sun-dried palms round a pool of brackish water.'

'It looks a long way from here,' observed Ginger.

'Roughly four hundred miles,' returned Biggles, folding the map. 'It will be nearly dark by the time we get there, but as it's the only green spot between here and French Equatorial Africa, it shouldn't be hard to find.'

In three minutes the Mosquito was in the air, climbing for height on a course due south, over what is generally acknowledged to be the most sterile area of land on earth. As soon as the altimeter* registered five thousand feet Biggles settled down to a steady cruising speed of three hundred miles an hour.

In an hour and a quarter by the watch on the instrument panel the oasis crept up over the southern horizon. In all that time the scene had remained unchanged—a flat, or sometimes corrugated, brown, waterless expanse, occasionally strewn with loose rock, and more often than not spotted with areas of lifeless-looking camel-thorn shrub. Nothing moved. The scene was as motionless as a picture.

'Is this oasis inhabited?' asked Ginger.

'I don't know for certain, but I should say it's most unlikely,' replied Biggles. 'Generally, only the very large oases have settled populations, although nomad Arabs on the move call anywhere if there is water to be had. Hallo! I can see something moving . . . a camel. Apparently there are Arabs here now.'

By this time the Mosquito was circling over the oasis, losing height as Biggles throttled back and put the machine in a glide. There was little to see. In shape, the oasis was roughly oval, perhaps a mile long and half that distance wide, set about with straggling palms. It appeared to stand on a slight eminence, with shallow wadis, or dry water-courses, radiating out at regular intervals. The sand lapped like an ocean, so that it was possible in one stride to step from a land of death to a fertile haven. There was no sign of aircraft. Near the centre there was a clearing in which had been erected what seemed to be a rough bough-shelter of dead palm fronds—a structure commonly found at oases.

*An instrument for indicating the height of the aircraft above the ground.

'It looks as if we've drawn blank,' muttered Biggles.

'I can't see anything,' said Ginger.

Biggles opened the throttle a little and continued to circle at about a hundred feet, all the time staring down at the depressing scene below. For some minutes nothing was said. Then Biggles remarked, in a curious voice, 'Is that a dead camel lying down there on the sand?'

'I see what you mean,' answered Ginger. 'I was just looking at it. It must be a camel, but it's a funny shape. What's that bundle of rags lying beside it—two bundles, in fact?'

'If the rags weren't so scattered I'd say they were dead Arabs,' mused Biggles. 'But why should Arabs die there, just outside the oasis? Where's that live camel?' He swung round towards the beast that was making its way slowly, and apparently with difficulty, towards the palms. 'From the way it's limping that poor brute has got a broken leg,' he went on sharply. 'What the deuce goes on here? I don't understand it at all.'

'Why not land and find out?' suggested Ginger.

'That's a practical suggestion,' acknowledged Biggles, and proceeded to adopt it.

As far as space was concerned there was no difficulty. On all sides between the wadis stretched the desert, flat, colourless, depressing in its dismal monotony. The sand, as far as it was possible to judge from the camel tracks, was firm. There was no wind, so choosing a line between two wadis that would allow the machine to finish its run reasonably close to the oasis, Biggles throttled back, lowered his wheels, glided in and touched down. The injured camel was about forty yards away, still limping towards the palms. Neither Biggles or Ginger paid much attention to it at the time. There was no reason why they should, for the risk of collision did not arise.

Just what happened after that—when Ginger was able to think again—was a matter of surmise. There was a blinding flash. With it came a thundering explosion. A blast of air hit the Mosquito and lifted it clean off the ground. For perhaps three seconds it hung in the atmosphere, at an angle to its original course, wallowing sickeningly. Then it settled down, struck the ground with one wheel, bounced, swerved, and came to rest with its tail cocked high.

Dazed, his ears ringing, in something like a panic Ginger pushed himself back from the instrument panel against which he had been flung, and tried to get out. The door had jammed. Biggles's voice cut in, it seemed from a distance.

'Sit tight,' he ordered.

Ginger looked at him and saw that he was removing a splinter of glass from his cheek. There was blood on his face. He looked shaken.

'What happened?' gasped Ginger.

'Nothing—only that we've landed in a mine-field,*' returned Biggles.

'Mine-field? What are you talking about?' ejaculated Ginger.

'Look at the camel—or what's left of it,' invited Biggles.

Ginger looked, and through the side window saw a

---

*An area full of buried mines, designed to explode at the pressure of someone walking or driving over where they are buried.

tangled mess of skin, hair, and blood, lying beside a shallow crater from which smoke was still rising sluggishly.

'That camel trod on a land mine; it couldn't have been anything else,' declared Biggles. 'The area must have been mined during the war, probably when the Italians were in occupation, and nobody has troubled to clear it up. A mine must have killed that other camel, and the two Bedouins*. This poor brute was probably with them, but got away with a broken leg.'

'That's beautiful,' muttered Ginger bitterly. 'It'll be a long time before this machine flies again—if it ever does. How are we going to get back? Thank goodness you told Algy to follow us. We can wait at the oasis. I—'

'Not so fast,' interrupted Biggles. 'You appear to have overlooked one or two details. The first is, between us and the oasis there is a hundred yards of sand under which, for a certainty, there are more mines. Personally, I've never walked through a mine-field; I've never had the slightest desire to do so, but it looks as if the time has come when I shall have to try it. Well, it'll be a new sensation. The second point that occurs to me is—supposing we are lucky enough to reach the oasis in one piece—what is going to happen when Algy arrives? He'll see the crash, and he'll promptly land. If he doesn't land on a mine he'll probably run over one as he taxies in—although the chances of that, of course, depend on how thickly the mines are sown.'

'We shall have to wave to keep him off,' suggested Ginger gloomily.

*Tent-dwelling nomadic Arab people.

'He'll probably think we're beckoning,' asserted Biggles. 'He's certain to land. We've been in some queer messes, but this one is, as the boys say, a fair knock-out.'

'What are we going to do?' demanded Ginger.

'I'll tell you what *you're* going to do,' answered Biggles. 'You're going to stay here. I'm going to the oasis.'

'But that's preposterous,' objected Ginger hotly.

'We should be very foolish indeed to walk together,' went on Biggles imperturbably. 'To start with, two pairs of feet would double the chances of striking a mine. If either of us stepped on one we should both go up in the air and come down in fragments, in which case there would be no one to tell the story. No, that won't do. Sitting here won't get us anywhere, so I may as well find a path to the oasis. That will be something to go on with. I can get half-way safely by stepping in the hoof marks of the camel. For the last fifty yards I shall have to take my chance. You'll sit here and have a grandstand view of the proceedings. If I get through, you can join me by following in my tracks. If I don't — well, follow my tracks till you come to the crater, then it will be your turn to take a chance.'

'And if we get to the oasis?' queried Ginger.

'We shall either have to work out some sort of signal to keep Algy off the ground, or poke about with sticks, like the sappers had to do in the war, to locate the mines. With luck—with a lot of luck—we may be able to mark out a runway and arrange a visual signal that will induce Algy to land on it. He'll have to land if we are to get home. One thing is quite certain; we can't walk it. We're four hundred miles from the nearest blade of grass, remember. Fortunately, we've plenty of time. Algy isn't likely to be along yet. I doubt if he'll get off the ground much before dawn. Well, it's no use messing about.'

As he finished speaking Biggles forced the door open and stepped out on to the sand. 'Don't move until you get the OK from me, then walk in my tracks,' he commanded.

The rim of the sun, a thin line of glowing crimson, was just sinking into the eternal wilderness. With its going, a veil of purple twilight was being drawn across the scene. Biggles turned towards the oasis.

With his heart in his mouth, as the saying is, Ginger leaned forward in his seat to watch. The strain was such that he found it difficult to breathe. He derived some slight relief when Biggles reached the tracks of the unfortunate camel, and then proceeded at a curious gait, imposed by the necessity of putting his feet in the oddly spaced hoof marks. The relief did not last long. Biggles reached the crater by the dead camel. He turned, waved, lit a cigarette, and then, to Ginger's utter consternation, strode casually towards the oasis as if he were out for an evening stroll.

Ginger held his breath. Knowing that every step Biggles took might be his last he watched with an agony of suspense that drove beads of perspiration through the skin of his forehead. He began to count the number of paces Biggles would have to take to reach safety—ten—nine—eight—

Chapter 9
Gontermann Makes A Proposal

Having reached the crater Biggles wasted no time — to use his own expression — messing about. Like a diver on a high board, the temptation was to hesitate; but this would be procrastination, and could avail him nothing. If a mine lay in his path, walking slowly would make no difference should he put his foot on it. So he walked normally. Nevertheless, he advanced with his eyes on the ground, seeking disturbed areas of sand that might betray the location of a mine. Long years of flying had taught him to be master of his nerves, so while the sensation was anything but pleasant he was not unduly perturbed, deriving a crumb of comfort from the knowledge that if he did step on a mine he would be unlikely to know anything about it.

In spite of all this it was with considerable satisfaction that he saw he had nearly reached his objective, the nearest point of the oasis, an area of coarse, wiry grass, from which the palms sprang. As he took the last pace, from the sand to the grass, a voice close at hand said, 'Congratulations.'

The sound, coming as it did in the hush of twilight, made Biggles start. He was utterly unprepared for it. Looking up, he saw, leaning against the bole of a palm in an attitude so elegant that it was obviously a pose, a man whom he had never seen before, but whom he recognised at once from photographs he had seen in the press. It was the tall, austere, good-looking ex-Nazi chief, Julius Gontermann, dressed immaculately as though for a ceremony in a tight-fitting, dove-grey suit of semi-military cut. Smoke spiralled from a cigarette in a long, gold-and-amber holder. His expression was one of cynical admiration and satisfaction.

He was not alone. Near at hand, in attitudes of idle interest, were Scaroni, Grindler, and Baumer, whom Biggles also recognised from his photograph. Grindler was the only one who openly displayed a weapon; he dangled an automatic from his trigger finger. There was one other man, a man whom Biggles certainly did not expect to see; but his presence explained the mystery of the third pilot. It was von Zoyton, a pilot — and, incidentally, an ace*—of the Luftwaffe, against whose *Jagdstaffel* he had fought a bitter duel over the Western Desert during the war.**

Von Zoyton smiled icy recognition.

Biggles shook his head sadly, and addressed him without malice, in English, which he knew von Zoyton spoke well.

'I'm surprised to see you mixed up in a graft like this. Perhaps you couldn't help being a Nazi, but you can help being a crook. I suppose they pulled you in because you knew the country?'

'Hit the nail right on the head, as usual,' conceded the German, who seemed amused about something.

---

*In the German Air Force, this meant a man who had shot down at least ten enemy aircraft.
**See Biggles Defends the Desert, published by Red Fox.

'Is there anything funny about this—or have I lost my sense of humour?' inquired Biggles.

'It is the winner's privilege to laugh,' answered von Zoyton. 'I've just won a hundred marks from Scaroni—who, by the way, produced and planted the fireworks. So proud was he of his effort that he laid me odds of ten to one that you wouldn't reach the oasis intact. I, gambling on your usual infernal luck, wagered that you would.'

'I'm glad you won your bet,' replied Biggles dryly.

Grindler interrupted with a snort. 'Say, what is this, a kids' party?' he snarled. 'If this guy's a cop I know how to handle him.'

'Plenty of time for that,' put in Gontermann. He, too, spoke in English, an affected, pedantic English, with an exaggerated Oxford accent through which ran an American drawl. 'I'd like a word with him first,' he added. 'Let's get up to the house. Come along, my dear Bigglesworth. Oh, by the way, you won't mind if I ask Baumer to take over any hardware you may be carrying—merely a precautionary measure against accidents, you know.'

Covered at close range by Grindler's gun, without a word Biggles passed over his automatic. Resistance, in the circumstances, was useless.

A short walk took them to the structure that Biggles had observed from the air, and he perceived at a glance that what he had seen was camouflage, clever camouflage, concealing a roomy, portable hutment of military design. The interior was simply but comfortably furnished, and illuminated by a hanging oil-lamp.

'Sit down my dear fellow,' invited Gontermann. 'May I offer you some hospitality? Get the drinks out,

Scaroni; our guest will be thirsty after his trying ordeal.'
He turned back to Biggles. 'You were foolish to come
here, you know.'

'Surely that remains to be seen?' returned Biggles
evenly.

Gontermann shrugged. 'What can you do? The age
of miracles has passed, my dear fellow.' He glanced
at Baumer. 'You'd better finish the business as we
arranged.'

As Baumer withdrew Biggles wondered what this
business was. He did not guess it.

'Now let us get down to what you English call, I
believe, brass tacks,' suggested Gontermann. 'There is
no need for me to tell you what we are doing here.
Conversely, we know what you are doing. Preuss is
rather a dull fellow, but he was able to find out. Are
we clear so far?'

'Quite clear,' agreed Biggles.

'In that case you must be wondering why we have
permitted you to go on living,' went on Gontermann,
smiling faintly.

'I must confess to some curiosity on the point,'
admitted Biggles, who, in actual fact, was thinking
of something quite different. He was wondering what
Ginger would make of his disappearance.

'An hour or two, more or less, is of no consequence
now that you are here,' said Gontermann lightly, pushing the cigarette box over to Biggles. 'I've heard about
you, of course. Your name was often mentioned in the
Wilhelmstrasse,* during the war, notably by my good

*Headquarters of the German Intelligence Service.

friend, Erich von Stalhein,* of the Gestapo. I gather you caused him a good deal of inconvenience?'

'I'm gratified to hear it,' murmured Biggles.

'Von Zoyton also had quite a lot to say about you,' continued Gontermann. 'And that brings me to the point of this interesting debate. You're the sort of man I should like to have with us. Our programme is going splendidly and there is no reason why it should not be expanded, if we can find suitable personnel. We can also do with one or two more machines, which, in your official capacity, you could acquire. You could also serve a useful purpose by keeping us informed as to the measures being taken against us.'

Incredulity puckered Biggles's forehead. 'Are you making this suggestion seriously?'

'Of course,' averred Gontermann. 'I'm not a man to waste time.'

Biggles sipped the drink that had been set before him, and lit a cigarette. 'You amaze me,' he said softly. 'You really do amaze me. Just as a matter of interest, what should I get out of this?'

'Money, my dear chap; and the satisfaction of exerting power over those who think they can run civilisation their own way for their own ends. The world is bursting with wealth. Why not have some of it? There are two sorts of people in the world, my dear Bigglesworth— the mugs and the others. The mugs accept what is doled out to them. The others, to which class we belong, help themselves. Here, take a look at these, for example.'

Gontermann picked up a black attaché-case, the

*See Biggles Flies East, Published by Red Fox.

property of the late courier, and carelessly tipped the contents on the table. Such a stream of jewels gushed forth that Biggles caught his breath in sheer admiration. There were ropes of pearls, strings of rubies, cut and uncut diamond and emerald rings and earrings, set as single stones and in clusters. Gontermann ran his fingers through the heap until it gleamed and flashed and flashed again as though illuminated by some unearthly fire.

'Pretty, eh?' he said slyly. 'Not bad, for a day's work? And there are plenty more where these came from.'

'I begin to see the force of your argument,' said Biggles slowly. 'But what', he went on, 'leads you to suppose, that having been allowed to leave here, I should not double-cross you?'

'That's my argument,' growled Grindler.

Gontermann ignored him. 'You would merely have to give me your word that you would not do so.'

'You'd accept that?'

'Of course. The word of a British military or civil servant is one of the few stable things left in a tottering world. Nevertheless, it is one of the weak spots in the British character, for it enables others, like myself, who have a more flexible code, to make our plans with a good deal of certainty. With men of your type, for instance, your word is a sort of fetish; you would suffer untold hardships, even die perhaps, rather than break it. Conditions in the world today, my dear fellow, do not justify such conceit. Give me your word that you accept my offer and you shall be as free as the vultures that otherwise will have the pleasure of dining on you.'

'Now I call that a really pretty speech,' sneered

Biggles. 'You have the brass face to sit there and accuse *me* of conceit, when —'

He broke off suddenly, as from outside came a sound which astonished him not a little, although a moment later, on secondary consideration, he realised that there was nothing remarkable about it. It was the sound of twin aero motors being started up.

'What's that?' he demanded.

'Only the Wolf, growling,' answered Gontermann with a smile. 'Baumer is about to give it a little exercise. He won't be long. You did not suppose that we had stranded ourselves here without air transport?'

'I hadn't thought about it,' returned Biggles, wondering how the machine, or machines, had been so cleverly camouflaged that his reconnaissance had not revealed them. 'What's Baumer going to do?'

'Finish the job you began so efficiently a few minutes ago. Your aircraft is rather conspicuous as it is. Being of wooden construction it should burn briskly.'

'But why use an aircraft to do that?' inquired Biggles.

'Because, my dear chap, the reaction of a land mine is precisely the same regardless of who treads on it. The area round this oasis is so thickly sown with mines that none of us feel inclined to use it as a promenade. There is, of course, a gap, known only to ourselves, for the purpose of taking our machines in and out.'

'Do you mean that Baumer is going to shoot the machine up?' cried Biggles, with a rising inflection in his voice.

'The only safe way to reach it is by air,' explained the German.

'But just a minute! He can't do that,' snapped Biggles. 'My second pilot is in it.'

'Ah! That's a pity,' murmured Gontermann smoothly. 'I'm afraid he is—how do you say?—out of luck. It's too late for us to do anything about it.'

This, clearly, was true, for the Wolf had already taken off, and now, to Biggles's unspeakable horror, came raking bursts of machine-gun fire.

'Stop him!' he shouted, and made a dash for the door.

Grindler raised his pistol, but Gontermann knocked it aside. 'Put that thing away,' he said irritably. 'You won't need it.'

Biggles went on until he had a clear view of the desert, and then stopped dead. The wrecked Mosquito was already enveloped in flames.

'Baumer is a very good pilot,' remarked Gontermann from his elbow.

Biggles started forward.

'Steady, Bigglesworth, steady,' said the Nazi. 'You can't do any good. Of course, if you choose to risk another trip across the mine-field I shouldn't dream of stopping you, but your luck might not be so good this time. At least give Scaroni a chance to recover his money with another little bet.' It was clear from the cynical banter in Gontermann's voice that he was thoroughly enjoying himself.

Biggles went on to the edge of the sand and then stopped. A wide area was lit up by the flames, but on it nothing moved. One thing was certain; anyone in the machine must already be a charred cinder. Gontermann had spoken an obvious truth when he had said, 'You can't do any good'. Biggles heard the Wolf land, but he did not see it. He could not take his eyes from what, he knew in his heart, must be Ginger's funeral

111

pyre. It was with difficulty that he maintained his composure. He had no intention of giving his enemies the satisfaction of seeing his distress.

'Well, I suppose it's no use staying here,' he said evenly.

'I hoped you'd see it in that light,' answered Gontermann. 'Come back to the mess and have another drink. That crude fellow Grindler is agitating to shoot you, but it has always been my policy to preserve anybody or anything that might be useful to me.'

They walked back to the hut. Baumer came in, with the air of a man who has done a good job. Biggles looked at him.

'You deliberately killed that boy,' he accused.

'Of course,' answered Baumer, quite casually. 'There was no point in leaving him out there to die of thirst. We had to burn the aircraft, anyhow. It might have been seen. He wasn't a relation of yours, was he?'

'No.' Biggles shook his head. 'No, he wasn't a relation. By the way, who shot down the diamond plane?'

'I did,' replied Baumer promptly, and with some pride.

'And the pay-roll plane from Nairobi?'

'Me,' Scaroni answered.

Biggles considered them with frosty, scornful eyes. 'It must be a source of infinite satisfaction to you, to know that you shot a couple of unarmed pilots through the back,' he said, with iron in his voice. 'Grindler murdered three men in the flying-boat—three quite ordinary fellows just doing their jobs. But there, he's used to that sort of thing. It seems he is in good company.'

Grindler rasped out a curse. Baumer started forward angrily, but Gontermann waved him back.

'As our guest, your remarks are not in the best of taste, my dear Bigglesworth,' he said suavely. 'It would be better to avoid personalities.'

'From your point of view, you are definitely right,' grated Biggles.

'This mine-field idea was a good one, don't you think?' went on Gontermann, switching the subject. 'That, and the desert, makes the oasis a perfect retreat, and at the same time, a prison that requires neither wire nor iron bars. Scaroni knew of the mines; indeed, he hid them when the British advanced during the war; but I take credit for putting them to practical use. Incidentally, Scaroni has some other useful equipment, too. By the way, should you go outside, keep away from the waterhole. The verge positively bristles with mines—a double row of them. You see, by this means, we have provided an almost unbreakable line of defence. Should anyone be so fortunate as to reach the oasis during our absence, which occurs from time to time, it is exceedingly unlikely that they would profit by it. After crossing the desert they would naturally make straight for the water, in which case . . .' Gontermann made a significant gesture.

Biggles flared up. 'That's a scandalous thing to do,' he protested hotly. 'What about the Arabs? They've probably used this oasis for centuries. They haven't harmed you.'

'Nevertheless, my dear fellow, they might be tempted to report what they had seen,' returned Gontermann casually. 'Besides, what is an Arab, more or less? You British are the most extraordinary people, always worrying about someone else. It impairs your efficiency. We do not allow ourselves to be hampered by such humanitarian scruples.'

'I've noticed it,' answered Biggles shortly.

'Well, what do you think of the scheme?' queried Gontermann.

Biggles did not answer. He was finding it hard to hold himself in hand. What had been a mere desire to bring these men to justice as a matter of duty, was now an obsession. The matter had become personal.

Gontermann hazarded a guess as to what was passing in his mind—and guessed wrong.

'I can give you until the morning to think it over,' he offered. 'We are leaving here at dawn. We use this place only occasionally, as an advanced landing-ground.'

Grindler broke in. 'What's that? Leaving here? Are we going back to that goldarned sanseviera?'

Gontermann flashed a scowl at him. 'Never mind where we're going,' he said curtly, and turned back to Biggles. He was smiling again, but Biggles could see that he was annoyed by Grindler's remark. 'Very well, my dear fellow,' he said airily. 'Let us leave it like that. The oasis is at your disposal. We sleep in the open—it's cooler. You can have a camp bed under the palms.'

Biggles raised his eyebrows. 'Aren't you going to tie me up or something?'

The German affected a look of reproach. 'To what purpose, old chap? If you feel like trying your luck again in the mine-field we shall be most interested spectators; but it is only fair to warn you, that in the unlikely event of your getting through, you would find the long walk across the desert to Sollum, without food

114

or water, rather exhausting. It's a good four hundred miles, you know. There's no cover, and we should find you quite easily. But why discuss it? I'm sure that you, with your reputation for intelligence, would not be so ill-advised as to attempt the impossible.'

Biggles did not argue.

'Just one other thing,' concluded Gontermann. 'At the moment there are two aeroplanes here. You would find them quite easily. They are in a slight depression under a sand-coloured awning. I mention this because you might be tempted to try your hand at the controls. Resist it. The ground around them is so thickly sown with mines that I confess to some nervousness every time I approach by the narrow path which was left for our accommodation. You'll forgive me if I don't show you the path?'

'I shall bear it in mind,' promised Biggles.

Chapter 10
Ginger Takes A Walk

Sitting in the cockpit of the Mosquito, Ginger had let out a gasp of relief when Biggles took the final step from the death-sown sand to the supposedly safe terrain of the oasis. He wiped the sweat from his forehead with a hand that trembled and sank back limply to recover.

Of course he kept his eyes on Biggles, expecting him to turn at any moment and give the OK signal. When this did not come he sat up again, not a little puzzled by Biggles's behaviour. There was no suggestion of a signal. Biggles was standing still, staring into the palms as though mesmerised. That in itself was odd. What was even more extraordinary, Biggles appeared to be talking to somebody—unless he was talking to himself, a most unlikely event. The trouble was it was nearly dark, and although some light was furnished by a rising moon, it was deceptive, and certainly not enough to probe the shadows of the palms.

When Biggles suddenly walked on and disappeared from sight Ginger was dumbfounded. He could not imagine anything that would have such an effect. It could hardly be possible that Biggles had forgotten him. Yet the fact remained, there was no signal. His orders on this point were clear. He was to remain in the aircraft until he received the OK to proceed. So he stayed, convinced that Biggles would presently reappear.

116

Minutes passed. Nothing happened. The oasis remained silent, with the deep stillness of death. The afterglow of the setting sun faded, and in the darkness that followed, the moon shone more brightly. Ginger continued to wrestle with a problem for which he could find no reasonable answer. If it seems strange that he did not guess the truth, it must be remembered that as a result of the air reconnaissance he had quite decided in his mind that the oasis was abandoned. So firmly had this conviction established itself that it remained unmoved. Nothing had happened to imply that he and Biggles might have been mistaken in their assumption.

But when, shortly afterwards, the clatter of aero engines being started up shattered the silence, he moved with alacrity, and with some agitation. For the obvious explanation of his problem did not come to him gently; rather did it burst upon him like a thunder-clap. The Renkells—or one of them—was at the oasis after all. If the machine was there, then it followed that the crew were there. Clearly, Biggles had walked into a trap, and that being so, it did not take Ginger long to decide that orders given before this fact was known were automatically cancelled.

As he jumped down on to the warm sand he saw the aircraft take off. It was not the transport, as he rather expected, but the Wolf, which suggested that the whole enemy party was at the oasis. It began to look very much as if the oasis was, in fact, the enemy's head-quarters. The Wolf, he observed, did not take off across the open sand; it chose for its run a shallow *wadi* that emerged from the eastern side of the oasis. Only too well aware that the sand was mined, Ginger guessed the reason. There was bound to be a gap in the mine-field, and the *wadi* provided it.

Actuated by this new peril, Ginger started running towards the *wadi* with the object of getting into the oasis. In his anxiety to discover what had become of Biggles he forgot all about such things as mines. Not until he was half-way to his objective did he remember them, and the effect produced was a sinking feeling in the stomach. But he did not stop. He daren't. In sheer desperation he ran flat out, and fairly flung himself over the rim of the *wadi*, where he lay panting, not so much from exertion as shock.

By this time the Wolf was in the air. He wondered where it was going, and why, so he lay still to watch. He could see it distinctly, for at no time was it more than a hundred feet from the ground, a performance that puzzled him considerably. Nor was his curiosity allayed when the machine banked steeply and came tearing back over its course. He wondered what it was going to do, for there appeared to be no reason for such an evolution.

What happened was the last thing he expected. The nose of the Wolf suddenly dipped in line with the Mosquito and a stream of tracer bullets* lacerated the sky, so that the sand round the damaged machine was torn and lashed with metal. Not all went into the sand, some must have penetrated the tank, for a flame shot up. Another minute and the machine was wrapped in fire. The bullets in the Mosquito's guns began to explode.

---

* Bullets loaded with phosphorus whose course through the air can be seen by day or night.

118

Ginger was about forty yards away—too close to be comfortable. He started running down the *wadi*. This, as he quickly realised, was a blunder, for in the light of the blazing aircraft the pilot of the Wolf saw him. This information was conveyed by a burst of bullets that sent him scrambling, flat on the ground, under the lee of a dune. The Wolf roared over him at a height of not more than ten feet, and then zoomed, as Ginger knew it must. He was also aware that the pilot would turn to confirm that he had hit his mark. Obviously, he must provide the pilot with a mark to shoot at. In a moment he had torn off his jacket, and flinging it down where he had been lying, made a dash for a clump of camel-thorn that clung to the side of the *wadi* at no great distance.

He reached it just as the Wolf completed its turn, and at once dropped its nose towards the jacket, which lay conspicuously on the open sand. Again came the vicious snarling of multiple machine-guns. In the lurid glow of the burning Mosquito Ginger saw his jacket leap into the air, and then go bowling down the *wadi* as though impelled by a jet of water from a pressure hose. With this he was quite content, thankful that he was not inside it. Had he been, he reflected, its spasmodic movements would have been much the same. He did not stir. From the flimsy cover of the leafless bushes he watched the pilot turn again and land, using the same *wadi* from which it had taken off. The machine taxied in. The clamour of its motors died away. There were a few odd noises, then silence fell. The glare of the burning Mosquito began to fade. Petrol-soaked wood and fabric burns quickly.

Ginger sat still long enough for the flames to die

down, and to recover from a series of shocks that had left him slightly bewildered; then he walked along the *wadi* to his jacket. It was shot to ribbons. With some difficulty he put it on, not so much because he wanted it as because he was loath to leave it where it might be seen in daylight, for this would expose his ruse. If the enemy wondered what had become of his body—well, they would have to wonder. He then returned to the camel-thorn to consider the situation.

His first inclination was to reconnoitre the oasis forthwith, approaching by the *wadi* which the Wolf had used as a runway, for this, as far as he knew, was the only safe passage. Desperate though the circumstances were, he had no desire to test his luck in the mine-field if it could be avoided. Then he remembered Algy and Bertie, who would be coming along in the Spur, and this threw him into a quandary. Although it was unlikely that they would arrive before dawn, there was a chance that they might turn up at any time. Even now they might be on the way. On arrival they would most certainly land, in which case the Spur would probably follow the Mosquito to destruction. If it were not blown up, it would probably be shot down by the Wolf in a surprise attack. That would not do. At all costs the Spur must be preserved, otherwise, whatever else happened, they would all eventually perish in the desert. The Spur was now the only link with civilisation.

Still pondering, Ginger also saw that even if the Spur delayed its flight until dawn, it would be futile to try to save it within sight of the oasis. If he stood up in the open desert where he could be seen by Algy, he would also be seen by the enemy. That would be fatal.

If it became known that he was still alive, steps would be taken to finish more efficiently the task the Wolf had just attempted. At present he was presumed dead, and if anything was to be done to save Biggles— assuming he was still alive—that impression must remain. He dare not risk going to the oasis to look for Biggles in case the Spur should arrive while he was there.

As far as he could see there was only one chance of saving the Spur, himself, and, eventually, Biggles. This was to go to meet the aircraft. Out of sight of the oasis he would be able to take up a position in a conspicuous place, where there was a fair chance that Algy would see him. Being the only moving thing in the desert he would stand out like a fly on a tablecloth. To make sure, he might even make smoke, for he had a box of matches in his pocket. If the machine came over before daylight he would have to light a fire, using such materials as were available. If Algy or Bertie failed to see him it would be just too bad, he decided. At all events, he would have done his best.

Feeling better now that he had a fixed plan, he turned his face towards the north, and started walking, keeping in the *wadi* for as long as it ran in the right direction. It gave him an uncomfortable feeling to recall that in front of him lay four hundred miles of desert. He had neither food nor water. It was better, he told himself, not to think about that. He knew all about the risks of becoming lost. Once before he had been lost in the wilderness, and he had no desire to repeat the experience. However, while the stars remained visible this should not happen. He walked on.

The moon climbed over its zenith, shedding an eerie

light over the vastness around him, and still he walked, a speck in the centre of a round horizon. An hour passed, and still there was the same circle of sand around him. He was tired, but he dare not rest in case he fell asleep, and the Spur passed over while he slumbered. In his hand he carried his matches, a few odd letters from his pocket, and some strips of rag torn from the lining of his jacket, all ready to make a tiny blaze should a drone in the northern sky herald the approach of the Spur.

An eternity of time passed—or so it seemed. Sometimes his feet sank into soft sand, sometimes they rustled harshly on rough volcanic ash. Once he crunched through an area of gleaming salt, evidently the dry bed of a lake. He tried talking to himself to keep awake, but the sound, in the empty loneliness, frightened him, and he soon gave it up. The night wore on. To his weary brain the outlook became ever more melancholy. He began to fear that even if he made contact with Algy and Bertie they would be too late to help Biggles. In the long night hours anything could have happened, he reflected gloomily.

More time passed. The moon ran its course across the heavens, and sank, as silently as a stone in a deep pool, into the distant world beyond the horizon. A period of darkness followed, and what with this, and sheer weariness, he was constrained to take a rest upon a little mound of sand. Around him the horizon was still the same unbroken circle, and a sinister feeling came over him that he was the only living creature left on earth.

But all things have an end, and for Ginger it came when the first faint flush of the false dawn lightened the eastern sky. The sun, of course, had not yet shown its face. Ginger stood up, and as he did so there reached his ears the sound for which he had so long waited— the drone of a high-flying aircraft. The sound came from the north, so that he knew it could only be made by the Spur. It was difficult to fix its precise position. But after a while, as he gazed up, he suddenly saw a living spark of fire moving across the dome of heaven. He had seen the phenomenon before, so he was not altogether surprised; but he was thrilled. He knew that the speck of orange light was a ray from the still invisible sun striking upwards, to be caught, and flung back, by the undersurfaces of the aircraft's wings. The world around him was still in sombre darkness.

In a moment, with fingers that shook a little from the knowledge of the tremendous consequences involved, he lighted his little fire. The flame of a match seized the paper hungrily, and devoured it all too quickly, almost before he could get the rag alight. He flung himself on his face and coaxed the flame with his breath. To his great relief the rag caught, but at best the fire was but a puny affair, and his heart went cold with apprehension. The plane droned on with awful deliberation through the crystal clear atmosphere.

Then came the daily miracle of dawn. First, the stars lost their brilliance. Then long pale fingers swept upwards, like beams from a battery of ghostly searchlights, to shed a mysterious radiance over the waste of sand. The light became tinged with colour, pink, green and gold. The colours faded, and it was day. The aircraft was no longer a spark, but a black speck speeding across a ceiling of eggshell blue.

Ginger threw up his arms and waved. He danced,

and ran about, hoping by this means to attract the attention of the pilot. And it seemed that he succeeded, for to his unspeakable joy the aircraft began to turn, and a change in the note of the engines told him that they had been throttled back. But he continued his gymnastics, swinging his tattered coat about his head, until he was convinced that he was the objective towards which the descending machine was heading. Then, quite exhausted by his efforts, and feeling rather foolish, he ran up and down the sand to make sure that it was firm, and that there were no obstructions such as rocks to spell final calamity.

The Spur landed, and it had hardly run to a standstill before he was on the wing, gesticulating, and making incoherent noises.

Bertie pushed back the lid*, and adjusting his monocle regarded him with frank alarm. 'I say, old boy, are you all right?' he inquired earnestly.

'No, far from it,' snapped Ginger, who was in no mood for pleasantries.

'You're not loony, or anything like that, from thirst?' queried Bertie.

'No!'

'Then what have you been doing to yourself? I've heard of people getting all worked up and rending their jolly old garments—'

'Never mind what you've heard,' broke in Ginger. 'Get out, both of you. I've got a tale to tell.'

Bertie jumped down, followed by Algy. 'What is it?' he asked anxiously.

'They've got Biggles,' announced Ginger.

---

* Slang: cockpit cover.

'Who's got him?'

'I don't know exactly,' confessed Ginger. 'Let me tell you all about it.' And he forthwith plunged into an account of the things that had befallen since the Mosquito left the coast.

'Beastly things, mines—if you know what I mean?' muttered Bertie when Ginger broke off.

Algy was still staring at Ginger. 'What in thunder are we going to do?'

Ginger shrugged helplessly. 'I don't know. I hadn't thought as far ahead as that. My one concern was to get hold of you.'

'How far are we from this perishing oasis?'

'I'm a bit hazy about that,' admitted Ginger. 'Somewhere between ten and twenty miles, for a rough guess.'

'If we fly over the place they'll see us,' went on Algy. 'If we land in that *wadi* they'll shoot us up as we come in, so that's no use. If we try to reach the oasis any other way we're liable to be blown up. Suffering Spitfires! What a kettle of fish.'

'We've got to do something,' declared Ginger.

'Absolutely . . . absolutely,' murmured Bertie, polishing his eyeglass.

'Don't stand there burbling like a bally parrot,' snarled Algy. 'Think of something.'

'How about shooting the beastly place up, and all that sort of thing?' suggested Bertie. 'Borrow some bombs from the boys in Egypt and fan the whole works flat. That would tear their rotten Renkells for them.'

'And tear Biggles at the same time,' grated Algy.

'By Jove! Yes, I didn't think of that,' confessed Bertie contritely. 'How about fetching some troops—punitive expedition, and so on, if you see what I mean?'

'And launch the attack somewhere about next Christmas?' sneered Algy, with biting sarcasm. 'Think again.'

'If we go on sitting here, the Wolf will probably come prowling along and find a nice sitting target,' muttered Ginger. He squatted on an undercarriage wheel and cupped his chin in his hands. 'We ought to be able to think of something. What would Biggles do in a case like this?'

Chapter 11
Biggles Takes To Water

Biggles passed one of the longest nights that he could recall. As Gontermann had promised he had been given a bed, actually a palliasse*, outside the hut; but he slept badly, if at all. As the night wore on, rather did he fall into a state of half oblivion, in which he was yet conscious of what was happening.

Ginger's presumed fate weighed heavily on him; indeed, it overshadowed everything, and, as is usual with death, created an atmosphere of unreality. Lying there, with nothing between his face and the stars, an immeasurable distance away, the drama seemed all the more poignant. The silence, too, was uncanny. Strain his ears, and listen though he would, everything seemed still and lifeless, as though he were alone on some forgotten world that had got adrift in space.

In spite of all that Gontermann had said, he could not believe that he was not being watched. If he was, he saw no sign of the watcher. Not that it mattered. He was content to lie and think. He wanted to think. He was worried about Algy and Bertie. Sooner or later they would arrive. Gontermann and his confederates knew nothing of that, but he did not see how he could turn their ignorance to advantage. The Spur would probably be blown up when it attempted to land. There

* A straw mattress.

appeared to be no way of preventing that. If he told Gontermann, it would come to the same thing in the end. On the face of it, nothing could prevent a melancholy conclusion to a mishandled affair. That the enemy was possessed of war stores, not normally available to civilians, and therefore unsuspected, was, to Biggles, no excuse. He could not shake off a feeling that he had shown a lamentable lack of foresight, with the result that he had blundered badly.

With the approach of dawn the air grew cooler. As the stars began to pale, unable to bear inaction any longer, he determined to find out if he was under surveillance. He was lying fully dressed, so the question of clothes did not arise. First he sat on the edge of the bed. Nothing happened, so he stood up. Still nothing happened, so with infinite caution he moved away among the palms, making no more noise than the moon passing across the heavens. At last the silence was broken by a curious sound that could only be described as a snort. Advancing in the direction whence it came he saw Scaroni, sitting with his back against a log, a rifle across his knees, as though he had been detailed to keep guard, but had dozed. Biggles eyed the rifle. It seemed too good to be true. But before he could move Scaroni started, yawned, and rubbed his eyes. It was clear that to attempt to get the rifle now would only result in a general alarm.

With no definite plan in mind, but hoping to make a discovery that could be turned to good account, Biggles edged away. Time was now important. At any moment the Spur might arrive, or Gontermann might appear to insist on an answer to his proposition, a proposition

which, Biggles knew quite well, was really an ulti-
matum. It was an issue he preferred to avoid.

He came upon the water-hole. Remembering the
mines, he regarded it from a safe distance. It was larger
than he expected—a silent pool of stagnant, dark-col-
oured water, of unknown depth, perhaps fifty yards
long and varying in width from twenty to thirty feet.
There were large patches of greenish scum, particularly
round the papyrus reeds that in several places fringed
the bank. He considered these reeds thoughtfully. They
were too sparse to offer a place of concealment even if
they could be reached; but as he gazed at them the
germ of an idea was born in his mind. At the far end
of the pool the palms straggled nearly to the edge of
the water. One had almost fallen, so that the trunk lay
far over, the sagging fronds hanging within three feet
of the placid surface of the pool.

This palm presented possibilities that Biggles was
not slow to observe. The trunk offered a passage, a
rather risky passage, by way of a bridge, over the mined
area surrounding the pool. Having reached the crown,
it should be possible, he thought, for a man to slide
down the fronds into the water without a great deal of
noise. It would be futile to suppose that anyone afloat
in the water would not be seen by a person standing
on the bank; but there was a trick . . .

His ruminations were interrupted by a cry. He recognised Scaroni's voice. The Italian shouted, 'He's gone!'
A moment later Gontermann answered: 'He can't have
gone far. See if you can find him.'

Biggles was already on the move. He did not need
to be told whom Scaroni was to find. There was this
about the situation; his fate, when he refused to join

the gang, was a foregone conclusion; so he stood to lose nothing by taking the most desperate risks to avoid a show-down.

In a moment he was astride the trunk of the fallen tree, working his way quickly towards the crown. His only fear was that Scaroni would arrive before he had accomplished his object, but apparently the Italian went first to the edge of the oasis to survey the desert, now grey with the advent of another day.

Reaching the crown, Biggles took a firm grip on one of the twenty-foot long fronds that hung nearly to the water, and lowered himself hand over hand to the extremity. The palm sagged under his weight, and as his feet touched the water he released his hold. The water at once closed over his head, which surprised him; he had not expected it would be so deep. He was pleased to find it so, for it suited his purpose. He swam into the nearest reeds. As these were stationed near the bank, the water shallowed, perhaps to a depth of three feet. The bottom was soft mud, which he was careful not to disturb. Breaking off a hollow reed, he took one end between his lips and sank under the water, leaving the other end of the reed clear. Through this improvised tube he was able to breathe, not easily, but for short periods of time without serious discomfort.

He did not really hope to get away with this simple ruse, which is practised by races practically all over the world. He was afraid Grindler would tumble to it, because in the old slave days of the United States it was brought to a fine art by escaping negroes, as the only efficacious way of eluding the hounds that were commonly employed to run them down. Biggles had often heard of the trick, but this was the first occasion he had attempted to put it into practice.

It had, he found, one big disadvantage—an obvious one. While under water it was impossible to see or hear what was going on outside, so to speak. He dare not look for fear of disturbing the water. A single ripple might betray him. He knew that his entry into the water must have caused some turbulence, but as time passed, and nothing happened, he had grounds for hope that the water had settled. The main difficulty was to keep submerged; his legs would float up, and it was only by clinging to the weeds that he was able to keep them down. Apart from that, he learned that he could not remain below the surface indefinitely; the strain was too great; it was necessary from time to time to take a deep breath. As nothing happened, this method of breathing became more frequent, and after a time he risked a cautious survey of the bank.

Not a soul was in sight, so he remained in this position, prepared to take cover should anyone appear. So long elapsed before this happened that he could only conclude that his enemies had left the pool out of account as a possible hiding-place, doubtless on account of the mines.

The sky was turning pink when Gontermann, Scaroni, and Grindler appeared, walking quickly, and having a lively altercation. Biggles dare not watch. With the reed in his teeth he sank quietly under water and waited. It was disconcerting, not knowing what was happening, but there was no way of getting over this without taking risks that hardly seemed justifiable.

He endured this final submersion for about five minutes. When he could stand the strain no longer he allowed his face to surface, slowly increasing his range of vision when no danger threatened. There was no one in sight. Gontermann and his accomplices had presumably walked right on. He supposed they were still looking for him, and derived some slight satisfaction from the knowledge that he was at least causing them some trouble. He now began to hope that they would think he had risked the mine-field, made a successful passage, and had fled into the desert.

He eased his position still more, going so far as to sit up, prepared, of course, to submerge instantly. Now that his ears were clear of the water he could hear voices. It sounded as if a violent argument was going on, with Grindler playing a major part. Biggles could imagine his wrath at the escape of the prisoner. This state of affairs persisted for several minutes, when he distinctly heard Gontermann say, in German, in a voice raised in anger, 'So! He's gone, but he will not get far. He will die in the desert. Say no more about it. Let us go.'

Voices continued to mutter, but very soon afterwards, they were lost in the roar of aero engines being started; and when, presently, the din was intensified, Biggles knew that both aircraft were about to leave. It became manifest that the bandits were sticking to their programme of departure regardless of the escape of their prisoner, although they might make a reconnaissance of the desert in the hope of spotting him on its bare surface. That is, if they got off. With a rifle it might be possible to do something . . .

At this juncture Biggles made a mistake, one that might well have had fatal results. So anxious was he to see what was going on that, forgetting the mines, he started to drag himself out of the water in the manner of a crocodile. Then he remembered, and with a grunt of disgust at his folly, he slid back. At the same time he perceived a contingency for which, in his haste to get into the pool, he had made no provision. How was he to get out? The frond from which he had dropped, which had sagged under his weight, was now far out of reach. With a shock he realised that he was, quite definitely, a prisoner in the pool—at any rate, for the time being.

While he was still occupied with this problem there was a roar as one of the Renkells took off. The other followed, and very soon he could see them both climbing into the blue. As he expected, they circled once or twice, evidently looking for him; then the transport straightened out and headed south-east, and soon afterwards the Wolf followed it.

With this state of affairs Biggles was well satisfied, even though his escape might only be temporary; for he realised that the departure of the aircraft, leaving him to his own devices, was not as casual as it might appear. From Gontermann's point of view, even discounting the mines, his complete escape from the oasis, surrounded as it was by four hundred miles of sand, must seem utterly impossible. This supposition was justifiable; no man, not even a Bedouin, could hope to make the journey. Only a fully equipped and properly provisioned expedition could traverse that awful wilderness without disaster. For the rest, the mines would take care of any casual visitors during the absence of the Renkells.

The drone of the aircraft died away.

Now that there was no longer any need for caution

Biggles directed himself entirely to the business of getting out of the pool, an operation which, with ample time, would present no great difficulty. But minutes, even seconds, were now of importance. The Spur might arrive at any moment, and if it landed in the minefield only a miracle could save it. Should the machine be wrecked, then he would be a prisoner indeed.

There was only one way of getting out of the pool, and that was by locating and clearing sufficient mines to form a gap. There was no alternative. He was glad Gontermann had stated specifically that there was a double circle of mines; this was valuable information; it meant that he had only to remove two mines in line to make a way through the circle.

He started work at the nearest point of land, digging with his hands. The sand, damp from the proximity of the water, was soft, and he made good progress. In five minutes his questing fingers had come in contact with the first metal instrument of death. It looked like two saucepan lids fixed face to face. He laid the mine on one side and proceeded. He hoped that the two rings of mines would be set close together, but in this he was disappointed, and he had to burrow a distance of four feet before he came upon the next one. The discovery gave him a nasty moment, for the mines were not in line, as he had supposed; they were staggered, making it impossible for anyone to reach the water. Should approaching feet by good fortune miss the first line, they would inevitably encounter the second. Unaware of this, he had been working with one elbow resting on the sand within an inch of the second mine.

He lifted the horror to one side, and with a deep breath of relief stood up to wipe the sweat from his face. He was in time. No distant drone had as yet announced the approach of the Spur. There was no need to hurry, so from his elevated position he made a casual survey of the oasis, or as much of it as could be seen. Not that he expected to see anyone. That was the last thing in his mind. Consequently, his nerves twitched with shock when a movement attracted his eyes.

He saw a figure sneaking towards the dust-coloured camouflage muslin under which the aircraft had been parked. Stalking would perhaps better describe the manner of approach. The figure was crawling swiftly from palm to palm. Already it was so close that Biggles realised it must be on the fringe of the mine-field which, according to Gontermann, surrounded the aircraft park.

For more reasons than one he nearly choked when the figure half turned, and he saw who it was. Oblivious to his own danger from further mines he dashed forward with a yell. 'Hi! Ginger! Stop!' he shouted.

Ginger stopped, staring, as well he might.

'For the love of Mike, don't move,' went on Biggles, still advancing. 'You're on the edge of a mine-field.'

There was no need to repeat the order. Ginger did not move. His jaw sagged. 'What—what shall I do?' he gulped.

'Retrace your steps, carefully.'

Ginger lost no time in acting on this advice. When he was at a safe distance he remarked, 'If there are mines about we had better warn Algy.'

Biggles blinked. 'Algy! Is *he* here?' He did not wait for an answer. Spinning round, he saw Algy advancing on a line that would take him to the pool. He let out another shout. 'Keep clear of that water!'

Algy backed away from the pool. Then, making a detour, he came to where the others were standing. He looked Biggles up and down.

'What in thunder have you been up to—having a mud bath?' he inquired.

'You bet I have,' answered Biggles grimly. 'I'll tell you all about it presently. How did you both get here? I thought Ginger was killed last night.'

'So did I,' admitted Ginger with a wry smile. 'But I shed my coat, and they shot that up instead.'

'But how did you both get into the oasis?' demanded Biggles in an amazed voice.

Ginger explained. 'I got away and made for the desert, heading north, to intercept the Spur. I lit a fire. Algy spotted it and came down. We talked the position over. I saw the Wolf take off last night, so I knew the way in and out of the oasis. We taxied the Spur into a *wadi* about five miles off, and leaving Bertie in charge, walked the rest of the way. We daren't taxi any nearer for fear of being heard. We were about a mile away when we saw the two Renkells go off; we lay flat until they were out of sight; we didn't know what was going on here. We came on to see. Are you here alone?'

'All by myself,' declared Biggles.

'Where's the gang?'

'Gone.'

Ginger shook his head. 'I don't get it. Why did they leave you here?'

'Sit down,' invited Biggles. 'I'll tell you.'

It did not take Biggles long to tell his story. When he had finished Algy asked: 'You don't know where these skunks have gone, then?'

'I haven't the remotest idea,' admitted Biggles.

'What do we do—wait here for them to come back?' put in Algy.

'I don't think we can do that,' replied Biggles. 'They may be away for weeks. It's hard to know what to do, and that's a fact. The difficulties of competing with air bandits become more apparent as we go on. In ordinary crime, a cop can shadow his man, no matter whether he travels by road, train, or steamer. On the ground there is always plenty of cover. You can't do that in the atmosphere because you have the sky to yourselves. Again, the ordinary detective usually has some idea of where to look for his man. At any rate, there are limits to the zone of operations. The people we're after have the whole blessed world at their disposal, and I'm just beginning to grasp what that means. The world is still a biggish place. I don't think Raymond realises what we're up against. It was fairly certain that the up-to-date crook would use aircraft, perhaps a private plane, to make a getaway. That's a different thing from this, which is sheer piracy; but whereas the old buccaneers ambled over the waves at a nice steady four knots, these blighters hit the breeze at four hundred miles an hour—which makes them rather more difficult to catch. I'm more than ever convinced that the best way, perhaps the only way, to stop this racket, is by finding the base aerodrome and wiping it out. That would cut off the petrol supply. But talking won't get us anywhere. We'd better bring Bertie here for a start. We can't leave him out there to fry in the sun. Algy, I think you'd better go; Ginger has done enough walking. You can fly back here in the machine. In the meanwhile we'll look for some breakfast. I imagine there is a food store here somewhere.'

'Okay,' agreed Algy. 'Watch where you're putting your feet. This place gives me the jitters. Every time I take a step I expect to hear a loud bang.'

'It isn't exactly the place to gambol about,' agreed Biggles, as Algy set off for the *wadi*.

It was getting on for three hours before Algy returned to where the others were waiting in a state of acute suspense. He came alone, on foot. He looked up at Biggles.

'He isn't there,' he said wearily.

'What do you mean?' asked Biggles sharply.

'What I mean is,' answered Algy, 'the machine's gone!'

Chapter 12

Bertie Flies Alone

Bertie was sitting under the port wing of the Spur, with his back against an undercarriage wheel, regarding the sea of sand around him with bored disfavour, when the distant drone of aircraft brought him scrambling to his feet with alacrity. For the sound came from the south, which could only mean that the Renkells were taking the air.

His first thought was for his own aircraft, and the subsequent events hinged on that factor. What had happened to Biggles, of course, he did not know. Algy and Ginger had gone to find out, and at that juncture the very last thing in his mind was to leave them marooned on the oasis. But he realised that if the Renkells were in the air he could not remain where he was, for should the Spur be spotted it would present a sitting target for the enemy to shoot to pieces at leisure. It was primarily in order to prevent this that he tore into the air, and then, prepared to give combat, edged away to the east into the cover provided by the blinding glare of the newly risen sun. This achieved, he surveyed the southern sky with the efficiency that comes of long practice.

His eyes soon found what they sought—two black specks climbing away from the oasis, which could now be seen, towards the south-east. The slight pressure of his right foot on the rudder-bar* was also automatic, and before he had seriously considered what he was doing he was in pursuit. At first, his intention was the natural one of shooting the machines down, or attempting to do so, to prevent their escape; and it was not until some seconds had passed that he perceived a serious objection to this course. It occurred to him, in the light of what Ginger had said, that Biggles might be a prisoner in one of the machines; indeed, if the Renkells were leaving the oasis this seemed highly probable—always assuming, of course, that the bandits had not killed Biggles out of hand. In view of this possibility it became obvious that aggressive tactics were, for the time being, at least, out of the question.

Still following the two machines, climbing for more height, but taking care to keep in line with the sun, Bertie observed further disconcerting prospects, factors that induced a state of indecision. If he shadowed the enemy aircraft, Algy and Ginger would certainly be left on the oasis without any means of getting away from it. On the other hand, if he abandoned the pursuit he might be throwing away a golden opportunity to discover what Biggles was most anxious to learn—the bandits' secret base. The fact that the Renkells were heading due south-east, on a dead straight course without any deviation, was significant; it seemed certain that they were making for a definite objective, and what could be more likely, he reasoned, than that this objective was their base depot? He made careful note of the compass course.

---

* Foot operated lever which the pilot uses to control the direction of flight.

Broadly speaking, Bertie's geography of the district was good, because he had served both in Egypt and Aden. He was aware, therefore, that if they held straight on they would come to the Anglo-Egyptian Sudan*. He was also aware that there was nothing but desert between their present position and the southern extremity of the River Nile. This was still some hundreds of miles away—precisely how far he did not know. It seemed unlikely that the Renkells would be going to the Sudan, and a vague idea formed in his mind that they were making for another oasis, perhaps at no great distance. So he decided to follow, telling himself that it would be an easy matter to return to the oasis when his object was achieved. Keeping as far away from his quarry as he dare without actually losing sight of them, he flew on.

An hour passed, and he began to get worried, for the Renkells were still streaking across the trackless blue as if they had no intention of stopping. Not that there was anything to stop for. At any moment Bertie expected to see an oasis creep up over the horizon, but this expectation did not materialise. Below, and on all sides, the sand rolled on, and on, and on, to more sand, and still more sand. There was nothing to indicate a boundary, but he knew they must now be over the fringe of the Western Sudan. Nothing changed; only the sun climbed higher, to strike down with shafts of white light at the winged invaders. The air quivered in the heat and the Spur rocked on an invisible swell. Even the engine seemed to moan.

Another hour passed. The sun climbed higher, the

* From 1898–1956 the Sudan was jointly governed by Egypt and Britain.

machine rocked, the engines moaned, and the frown that lined Bertie's forehead deepened. Where was this crazy chase going to end? Had he known that it was to last as long as this he would have thought twice about following, he reflected bitterly. They had now covered some six hundred miles, and he looked more often at his petrol gauge. He was alarmed at the thought of going on, yet he dare not turn back. True, he still had enough petrol to reach the oasis, but that was not enough. It was no use arriving back at Zufra with an empty tank. There would be another four hundred miles to cover—the distance between the oasis and the North African coast, the nearest point of civilisation. Already he had overstepped the margin of reasonable safety for such a trip—a trip on which it would be the height of folly to risk a forced landing. So he went on, not a little worried, with an increasing conviction that he had behaved rashly, to say the least of it.

Another hour passed. The sun climbed into its throne; the machine rocked sickeningly in the tortured air, and still the desert rolled away on all sides, to eternity, it seemed. The Spur was like a fly hanging over the centre of an enormous bowl, a bowl of gleaming sand. The heat was terrific, and as so often happens in such conditions, a haze, a deceptive invisible haze, began to form. The hard line of the horizon became a distorted blur, and at the risk of being seen Bertie had to close up with his quarry to avoid losing them. If either of the enemy crews saw him they gave no sign of it.

The Spur's petrol was now so low that it was with heartfelt relief that Bertie observed a ragged fringe of palms across his bows. As he drew nearer, a broad river, which he knew could only be the Nile, came into view. He had only a very vague idea of what part of the river it was, but that, for the moment, did not matter. It was pleasant to see again something green. Now, surely, the Renkells would go down.

The Renkells went on. Bertie glared; he muttered; but it made no difference. To give up the pursuit, after such an extended chase, would be maddening, but prudence counselled a halt while there was still a little petrol in the Spur's tank. He wavered, and while he did so his problem was answered for him. The Renkells, still on their original course, disappeared into the haze. Bertie made a half-hearted attempt to find them, but he soon gave it up. Just what lay ahead he did not know—except, as far as he could see, the desert. Clearly, it would be suicidal to go on. The Spur had been handicapped in the matter of range by starting from the coast with a tank that was not full. Then there had been the flight to Zufra, which had lowered the gauge still more. The Renkells had obviously started from the oasis with full tanks, which suggested that petrol, probably in a concealed dump, was available at Zufra. Bertie made a mental note of it, and turned back to the river, over which he had passed.

Hot, tired, and, disgruntled, he followed its course northward, and was pleasantly surprised when, after a further twenty minutes in the air, he saw a town of flat roofs that he recognised as Khartoum, with its aerodrome and big R.A.F. depot. Down to the last pint of petrol, he landed, and reported to the duty officer, a youthful pilot officer who, judging from his manner, regarded him with not unpardonable suspicion.

143

'What cheer,' he greeted.

'What cheer yourself,' returned Bertie.

The lad looked at the Spur. 'That isn't the sort of machine I'd expect a civilian to be flying,' he observed shrewdly.

Bertie considered him through his monocle with sympathetic toleration. 'In this world, a lot of things will happen that you don't expect, young feller-me-lad,' he responded. 'I'd like some petrol—and all that sort of thing.'

'Is that so?' inquired the duty officer, sarcasm creeping into his voice. 'What do you think this is—a public garage?'

'I,' said Bertie deliberately, 'am a policeman.'

The pilot looked incredulous. 'Are you kidding?'

Bertie frowned. 'Don't I look like one?'

The lad looked Bertie up and down. 'No. In fact, I can't recall ever seeing anything less like one,' he remarked, with the ingenuous frankness of youth. 'Got any papers on you?'

With mild consternation Bertie realised that he had not—or none that would help him. Biggles carried the official documents. He made this confession.

'You're coming with me to see the C.O.,*' decided the duty officer, with some asperity.

'All right—all right—there's nothing to get excited about,' returned Bertie. 'Who's in command here?'

'Group Captain Wilkinson.'

'Not the chap they call Wilks?'

'That's him.'

'That's   marvellous — absolutely   marvellous,'

*Commanding Officer.

144

murmured Bertie. 'Astonishing luck, and all that. My troubles are over.'

'Is he a pal of yours?' inquired the pilot.

'No—but he's a pal of mine*—if you see what I mean?' declared Bertie.

'I don't, but never mind. You can tell your hard luck story to him,' consented the pilot. 'But I warn you,' he added, 'he takes a poor view of aviators who waffle about the Sahara with dry tanks. Come on.'

In a few minutes, having introduced himself, Bertie was telling his story—or as much of it as was appropriate—to the Group Captain, whom he had never met, but whom he knew had for years been a close friend of Biggles, who always referred to him as Wilks.

'Well, well. So Biggles is an airborne cop?' murmured Wilks when Bertie had finished. 'He's tried most things, but this is something new. And you say you don't know where he is?'

'If he wasn't in one of those two Nazi kites, then he's still at Zufra—alive or dead,' answered Bertie.

'It would surprise me very much if he were dead,' returned Wilks, with a faint smile. 'By rights he should have been killed years ago, but he seems to be one of those chaps who have the knack of slipping through the clammy clutches of Old Man Death every time. But what's your idea now—I mean, what do you propose doing?'

'There's only one thing I can do,' decided Bertie. 'If you'll fill me up with juice I'll claw my way back to Zufra and have a dekko round the jolly old date palms.'

Wilks looked serious. 'You can have the petrol, of

*See Biggles and the Fighter Squadron, published by Red Fox.

course, but it seems to me that there are several snags in that arrangement. First of all, it's bad country, and there's a deuce of a lot of it between here and Zufra.'

'I noticed it,' murmured Bertie.

'Down here we don't like machines flying alone too far afield,' went on Wilks. 'We prefer to fly in pairs, at least, the idea being that if one has trouble, and has to go down the other can pick him up, or pin-point the spot so that we know just where he is. Another snag; you say Algy Lacey and young Ginger Hebblethwaite are at Zufra. If Biggles is there, there will be four of you. You couldn't all pile into the Spur. You would have to make at least two journeys to get them out. I can't see any necessity for that. Why not take a big machine, or better still, have one of my Lankies* go along with you. You could then evacuate the whole party at one go.'

'That's a stupendous idea—absolutely terrific,' declared Bertie. 'Jolly sporting of you, and all that.'

'I'm a bit worried about these mines,' went on Wilks. 'We can't leave the infernal things lying about for the Arabs to trip over. They'll have to be cleared up.'

'Absolutely,' agreed Bertie. 'But not by me. No bally fear. I'm frightened to death of the beastly things.'

'I wasn't thinking of you,' replied Wilks. 'I'll have a word with the political officer about it. It's really his

---

*R.A.F. slang for the Lancaster Bomber.

pigeon. We've got some Askaris* here—the Fourth Pioneer Corps. They are trained in mine detecting—had
plenty of practice chasing Rommel in the Western
Desert during the war. They could go out in the Lanky
when you go.'

'Absolutely. By Jove! Yes,' said Bertie, warmly.
'Then, if the crooks were still in occupation at Zufra
we could mop the whole place up—what!'

'I'll suggest it to headquarters at Cairo,' promised
Wilks. 'We should have to get their okay. I'll tell you
what. Leave this to me. You trot along to the mess**
and tear open a tin of bully. By the time you get back
I shall have got a decision on the matter. If it's okay
to proceed I'll organise the sortie.'

'That's the tops, sir, absolutely tophole,' declared
Bertie. 'Biggles always said you were the king-pin.
Thanks, and all that.' Feeling better, Bertie went off to
the mess.

When he returned, an hour later, he found that the
station commander had wasted no time in keeping his
promise. With him was a flying-officer, and a spick and
span, dark-skinned, Askari sergeant.

Wilks introduced the R.A.F. officer. 'This is Collingwood,' he said. 'Colly, for short. He'll fly the Lanky.
Unfortunately, Jones of the Askaris is down with fever,
so I got in touch with Cairo myself. They say the mines

*The Pioneer Corps is probably the most polyglot corps in the world.
Commanded by English officers, the rank and file are nearly all African—Libyan Arabs, Nubians, Sudanese, and a host of other nationalities. These men are commonly called Askaris (from Arabic-French *askar*,
meaning an army). They love the drill and ceremony of soldiering, and
it is not an uncommon sight to see one, in his spare time, drilling
himself, shouting his own commands.
**The place where officers eat their meals and relax together.

147

must be cleared immediately, and the Fourth Pioneers are to do the job. They'll take mine-detecting gear with them, and stay at Zufra till the work's finished. It'll probably take two or three days. I've told Collingwood that there's no need for him to stay there; Sergeant Mahmud is quite capable of taking charge. Colly will go back in a day or two to bring the working party home. If you can show Sergeant Mahmud roughly where the mines are, he'll do the rest.'

'I'm not sure about the position of the mines myself, but Ginger knows all about them,' remarked Bertie.

'In that case you'd better land both the Spur and the Lanky well clear of the oasis, and march in,' suggested Wilks.

'Absolutely,' agreed Bertie, emphatically.

'If you do happen to meet any opposition at Zufra the Askaris will handle it—not that I think that's likely, since the Renkells have fled elsewhere.'

Bertie concurred.

'If Biggles is at Zufra, with the others you could all come back here together,' went on Wilks. 'As the crooks have gone somewhere south-east of here I imagine that this place would suit you as well as anywhere for a temporary base.'

'That's what I was thinking,' rejoined Bertie. 'The final decision about that, though, will rest with Biggles, if he is still at Zufra.'

Wilks nodded. 'Good enough. Your machine has been refuelled, so you may as well get off right away. That should get you to Zufra before sundown. You could either come straight back here or wait till morning. There's a moon, so if you take my tip you'll make a night flight—it's a lot more comfortable than flying across that devil's cauldron in the sun.'

'I'll remember it, and thanks again for your co-operation. It makes it all easy.' Bertie turned to Colly. 'I'm ready to push off, if you are.'

They went out to the aerodrome, where Bertie watched a dozen efficient-looking Askaris, under Sergeant Mahmud, in full desert equipment, file into a Lancaster that stood waiting. Colly climbed into his cockpit. As the motors growled Bertie walked over to the Spur.

In a few minutes both machines were off the ground, thrusting north-west through the sun-drenched air above the scintillating sea of sand.

Chapter 13
Events At El Zufra

It did not take those left at the oasis long to force the door of the hut and help themselves to the ample supply of tinned food and mineral waters which they found there. Their immediate requirements satisfied, they selected a shady position under the palms, one that commanded a view of the desert to the north, and sat down to wait for what might befall. There was nothing else they could do.

Naturally, their conversation was practically confined to one subject — the mystery of Bertie's disappearance. Algy stated positively that the Spur had not been attacked on the ground, or there would have been evidence of it, such as bullet-marks in the sand, which he could not have overlooked. After debating the subject from all angles they were unanimous in the opinion that the most obvious solution was probably the correct one — that Bertie had seen or heard the Renkells take off, and had followed them. Biggles asserted that he could think of no other reason why Bertie should leave the ground.

As the day wore on, what did puzzle him was why the Spur should remain away for so long. It gave rise to a fear — although he did not mention this — that Bertie had attacked the Renkells, found trouble, and was down somewhere in the desert. When four hours had elapsed, and still the Spur did not show up, he inclined more and more to this view. Knowing the endurance of the aircraft, he remarked that wherever the machine might be, it was no longer in the air, for the simple reason that its petrol must be exhausted.

'One thing is quite certain,' he averred. 'We can't get back on our feet. Four hundred miles would be a tidy jaunt on a macadam road with a tavern at every corner. Across that'—he nodded towards the glowing sand—'it couldn't be done. Gontermann was right about that. The only thing we can do is wait. If the Spur doesn't come back, then we'll stay here and fight it out with the crooks when they return, as they are almost sure to, sooner or later. If the Spur does come we can't all get into it. I'll fly up to Egypt with Bertie and try to get another Mosquito to replace the one we've lost. Which reminds me: if Bertie comes back he won't dare to land near the oasis for fear of putting his wheels on a mine. The chances are that he'll land at the place from which he took off. He knows that's safe, and that's where we shall look for him. But we can't sit out there all day in the sun. One of us will have to go out and leave a note to let him know that we're waiting here, at the oasis. If we fix it on a piece of stick he can hardly miss seeing it. We'll tell him to taxi towards the *wadi*, when one of us will go out to show him the way in.'

'He knows there's a safe runway along the *wadi*, because I told him so,' put in Ginger.

'Never mind. We'll go out to meet him. This is no time to take chances,' asserted Biggles.

'What beats me is, why the Renkells left here, and where they could have gone,' muttered Algy.

'They probably left here because it's no sort of place

for an extended stay,' answered Biggles. 'They only use the oasis as an advanced landing-ground; they told me so; which means that their permanent hide-out is tucked away still farther in the back of beyond.'

'When they talked about leaving in the morning, they didn't drop any sort of hint as to where they might be going?' queried Ginger.

'Come to think of it, they did—or rather Grindler did,' murmured Biggles thoughtfully. 'I can't remember his exact words, but he said something about going back to that goldarned Sanseviera—or some such word. It sounds like the name of a place. I've never heard of it, but if it is, we ought to be able to find it. Now I think we ought to see about fixing that note in case Bertie comes back.'

'I'll take it,' offered Ginger. 'This sitting here doing nothing gives me the willies.'

'Be careful not to lose your way—it's pretty hot out on the sand,' warned Biggles.

'Don't you worry about that,' returned Ginger grimly. 'I shall follow our tracks out and back. You write the note.'

Biggles wrote the message on a leaf of his note-book, and selecting a dead palm frond, stripped it until only the spine remained. In the end of this he made a slit to hold the paper, and passed it to Ginger, who took it, and with his tattered jacket on his head departed on his errand.

Biggles and Algy sat in the shade where they could watch him, still talking over the strange turn of events, grim evidence of which lay before them in the shape of two dead Arabs, the remains of two camels, and the blackened area that marked the burnt-out Mosquito.

None of these could be approached, of course, on account of the mines.

Time passed, probably the best part of two hours. They saw Ginger coming back, a microscopic figure in the vastness, making for the entrance to the *wadi* which, as far as they knew, provided the only safe path through the mine-field. They watched him without any particular interest; and perhaps because their eyes were on him they failed for some time to see another movement away to the west. In fact, their attention was only called to it by the behaviour of Ginger, who suddenly stopped, staring across the sand, shielding his eyes with his hands. At that time he was about four hundred yards away.

'What's he staring at?' muttered Algy, with quickening interest.

Biggles uttered an ejaculation and sprang to his feet. He did not speak. There was no need. Also advancing towards the oasis, on a line that would intercept Ginger before he reached it, from a fold in the ground had appeared a group of camels, mostly with riders, a dozen all told, with long rifles slung across their shoulders.

'Arabs,' said Algy.

'Touregs,' said Biggles, noting the blue veils that covered the faces of the riders. There was a suspicion of uneasiness in his voice, for he knew that while the nomad Touregs seldom interfered with travellers, they resented their intrusion, and on that account were not entirely to be trusted. Still, he did not think they were in real danger. Neither, evidently, did Ginger, for after a good look at the newcomers he walked on towards the oasis.

Biggles's only real fear at this stage of the proceed-

153

ings was that the Touregs might inadvertently attempt to cross the mine-field; not for a moment did it occur to him that they might know about the mines; and it was with the object of preventing an accident that he started forward. At the same time the riders whipped their camels into a run, directly towards Ginger who, seeing that he was their objective, stopped to wait for them. In any case he could not hope to outrun the camels to the oasis. Wild yells from the Touregs now made it plain that their intentions were not friendly.

'You stay here, Algy,' snapped Biggles, and began running along the *wadi* towards the group out in the desert.

By the time he had reached it Ginger had been surrounded, and was now being driven in a hostile manner towards the oasis.

The party halted and silence fell as Biggles ran up, hands raised to show that he was unarmed. Dark, sullen, inscrutable eyes, looked down on him. He spoke first in English, but receiving no answer, tried French. Upon this, at a word of command, one of the camels couched*, and its rider, a leader by his bearing, dismounted. He was tall, bearded, lean, with fierce eyes, a true son of the desert and a magnificent specimen of manhood. He answered Biggles, in guttural French, with a question.

'Why have you done this?' he demanded harshly, indicating the desert with a sweep of his arm.

At first Biggles did not understand. Then he saw the Touregs looking at the dead men and beasts that lay drying in the sun, and it needed no effort of the

*Sat down to enable its rider to dismount.

154

imagination to guess the cause of the Touregs' belliger-
ent attitude.

'We did not kill them,' he said quickly.

'You have put bombs in the sand,' accused the
sheikh.

All was now plain. 'These men who were killed were
of your tribe?' queried Biggles.

'One was my son,' was the grim rejoinder. 'My
brother lost an arm, but was able to reach my tents.
You fired at him with rifles as he ran across the sand.'

This was worse, much worse, than Biggles expected.
He did not doubt that the chief spoke the truth, and
he mentally cursed Gontermann for his foul work.

'We did not shoot, and we did not put bombs in the
sand,' he asserted. 'Not knowing that you knew of the
bombs I ran out to warn you not to cross the sand.
The men who did this evil thing are our enemies; we
came here seeking them; that, O sheikh, is the truth,
and the government at Cairo will bear witness.'

The Toureg's hard expression did not change. 'What
does it matter who put the bombs? The faces of the
men who did this thing were white, so they were of
your tribe.'

Biggles realised the futility of trying to explain that
all white men were not of the same 'tribe.' 'There are
bad men, and good, in every tribe,' he said earnestly.
'The men who put these bombs in the sand are outlaws,
fleeing from justice. They tried to kill us, too, but we
escaped.'

The sheikh was not impressed. 'Where are your
camels?'

'We have no camels,' answered Biggles.

'Then how did you get here?'

'We came through the air in one of the machines that fly.'

The sheikh drew in his breath with a hissing sound, and there was a note of triumph in his voice when he challenged. 'The men who put the bombs came here in a flying-machine. You must be the same. Allah, the Merciful, has delivered you into our hands. We shall kill you. Go.' The chief pointed to the oasis.

'Wait!' cried Biggles. 'I say again that the men who put the bombs in the sand were our enemies, enemies that we came here to seek. If you kill us they will go free, for you cannot follow them into the air. We are your friends, and to prove this I warn you that when you reach the oasis, keep away from the water, for there are more bombs in the sand around it. Stay away, too, from the large tent, where there are yet more bombs; but this, I swear, was not our doing.'

'What does it matter who did it?' returned the sheikh with simple but deadly logic. 'My son is slain. White men are all the same. They bring death to where there was only peace.'

Biggles looked at Ginger and shrugged his shoulders. 'I'm afraid there's nothing we can do about it. I sympathise with these chaps. We can't blame them for taking this line. Were we in their sandals we should probably feel the same way as they do about it.' To the sheikh he said, 'Keep in the *wadi*; it is the only safe way.' And with that, followed by the rest, he walked back to the oasis.

Algy was waiting at the fringe, his right hand behind his back. Knowing that it held a pistol—he himself was unarmed—Biggles shook his head. 'Put it away,' he said quietly. 'If you show it it will only make matters worse. We can't fight this bunch. Our only hope is to try to placate them by argument. They think we laid the mines—the sheikh's son was killed by one.'

Algy returned the pistol to his pocket. 'May the devil run away with that hound Gontermann,' he snarled. 'One skunk like that undoes all the good our people do.' He joined the party, which proceeded to an open area among the palms, close to the water-hole.

There was nearly a nasty accident forthwith, for the camels strained to get to the water, and it was only with difficulty that they were held back. Biggles shouted, and pointed to the two mines which he had unearthed, as proof of his allegation that the pool was a death-trap.

'If you need water I'll fetch it for you,' he offered. And he did, in fact, fill the Touregs' leather buckets and water-skins, going to and fro through the narrow path he had cleared to escape from the pool. The tribesmen watched him with cold, expressionless eyes.

When the camels had been watered and tethered the Touregs formed a rough circle in the clearing, and the sheikh addressed them in their own tongue. It was a long speech. No one interrupted. What he said, of course, the prisoners did not know, although it was obvious that their fate was being discussed. They sat together, watching, Biggles smoking a cigarette. The question of escape did not arise, for there was nowhere to go except into the desert, which offered only an alternative form of death. The Touregs were well aware of this and took no notice of them.

When the sheikh finished talking the others at once broke into a violent argument among themselves—or so it appeared.

'I wish I knew what was going on,' muttered Ginger.

'I think it's pretty clear,' replied Biggles. 'The sheikh has told the story of the mines, with all the gory details, after the manner of a judge summing up. He has now left it to his men to decide what shall be done with us. That's the usual Arab way of doing things. The sheikh's own opinion no doubt carries a good deal of weight, but with these wandering bands it isn't final. A man is chosen as chief, but he only holds that position while the majority agree with him. The true Arabs refuse to be dictated to by anyone; they obey their chief as long as it suits them; but if they disagree with him they get over the difficulty by choosing another sheikh. The fact that these fellows are arguing is a good sign. It means that some of them, including the sheikh, I fancy, are against doing anything drastic in a hurry.'

At this point the sheikh came up to Biggles and asked, 'Where is the machine that flies?'

Biggles stretched a finger towards the charred remains of the Mosquito. 'Our enemies, your enemies, those who put the bombs in the sand, set fire to it and fled, leaving us to perish, as you may see for yourselves.'

The sheikh obviously repeated this information to his men, and it seemed to make a good impression. As Biggles had said, the point of his argument was there, on the sand, for all to see.

Biggles decided to follow up the ground he had gained. He addressed the sheikh. 'If you kill us,' said he, 'the bombs will remain in the sand for all time, and the oasis will be a place of death for every Arab who passes this way. Help us to cross the desert and we will return with soldiers who will clear away the bombs and make the place safe for man and beast. *W'allah!* It is for you to decide.'

The sheikh repeated this statement, again with good effect, for the advantages of the plan to the Arabs could hardly be denied. Only one or two of the warriors were irreconcilable, handling the hilts of their long-bladed knives in a manner that left no doubt as to the course they would have preferred. Nevertheless, they were a minority; the chief harangued them, and Biggles ventured to predict that everything would be all right.

And so it might have been but for a tragedy that overwhelmed all the good that had been gained by fair argument. One of the warriors, moved by some impulse known only to himself, strode towards the water-hole. No one noticed him for a moment. Then Biggles caught sight of him out of the corner of his eye and let out a yell, but he was too late by a split second. The shout was lost in a deafening explosion that threw everyone flat. The man who had stepped on the mine lay where he had been flung, a horrid heap of quivering flesh. Another warrior was trying with his hands to stop blood that was spurting from his leg. Another clutched at his face, that had been torn open by a splinter.

Silence fell—a deadly, ominous silence.

'That, I'm afraid, has sunk us,' remarked Biggles evenly.

The Touregs, for a moment stricken dumb by shock, found their tongues in a howl of rage. There was no longer any talking, only fierce muttering. All eyes were on the prisoners. Knives swished from their leather sheaths. Only the sheikh stood aloof. The circle began to close in, not quickly, but slowly, as though there was some doubt as to who should strike the first blow.

'This is it,' said Algy, and drew his pistol.

'I object to being butchered like a sheep,' declared Ginger. He, too, drew his automatic.

The Touregs halted, tense, some half crouching, checked for the moment. The atmosphere was electric, like the lull before a storm.

Chapter 14

Back To The Trail

Into this dramatic scene anticlimax arrived like a thunderbolt—although with less noise.

'Hi! Hi! Hi! there,' said a voice in a tone of gentle reproof. 'You fellows mustn't do that sort of thing, really, you know.'

Again silence fell. All movement stopped except at one place. Bertie, monocle in his eye, a cigarette between his lips, smiling a rather foolish, almost an apologetic grin, walked slowly into the scene as an actor steps on a stage from the wings. He tapped the ash off his cigarette. 'Hallo everybody,' he greeted. 'Sorry I've been away so long. It looks as if I've arrived in the jolly old nick of time—what?'

'You've arrived just in time to get your jolly old throat cut,' muttered Ginger.

Bertie stopped. 'Really? I say, that's too bad.'

'Don't stand there looking like a fool,' grated Biggles. 'There's going to be a rough house.'

The Touregs stared at Bertie. They stared at Biggles. They stared at each other, dull amazement on their faces. Bertie's miraculous arrival evidently upset them. It may have been the calm manner of it as much as the actual event. At any rate, shock took the sting out of them, if only temporarily. The sheikh spoke to Biggles, pointing at Bertie.

'Who is this man who wears a window in his face? Is he your friend, or an enemy?'

'A friend,' answered Biggles.

'Is he alone?'

It did not occur to Biggles that this could be otherwise, but he put the question to Bertie.

'Alone? No bally fear,' answered Bertie. 'We're quite a party. You wait and see. I walked on ahead.'

There came a sound of voices, and a moment later another actor appeared on this curious stage. It was Flying-Officer Collingwood, in uniform.

'What cheer,' he said casually. 'What's going on?' He glanced at the Touregs. 'You've got company, I see.'

Before anyone could answer Sergeant Mahmud and his twelve Askaris appeared at the edge of the clearing. They halted, and at a word of command, 'ordered arms' smartly. The comical part of this was, that after a curt nod of greeting to the sheikh, Sergeant Mahmud took no further notice of the Touregs, who, suddenly confronted by this display of armed force, continued to stand and stare. One by one they sheathed their knives.

Biggles shared in their surprise. He, too, stared, mostly at the Askaris. 'Bertie, where in heaven's name did you pick up this army?' he asked in a dazed voice.

'Pick it up? I didn't pick it up,' declared Bertie. 'The Higher Command has sent them along to clear up these beastly mines.'

Biggles passed a hand over his eyes like a man who doubts his senses. 'Where the deuce have you been?'

'Khartoum,' answered Bertie evenly.

Biggles started. '*Where?*'

162

'Khartoum. You know, the jolly little place on the Nile.'

'But that's a thousand miles away.'

Bertie smiled wearily. 'It seemed more like ten thousand to me—I've just been there and back.'

Biggles leaned limply against a palm. 'I'm going crazy,' he muttered. 'It must be the sun.'

'I wasn't sure about the mines, so we parked our kites on the sand and walked in.'

'Kites?' queried Biggles. 'Don't tell me you've brought a squadron here?'

'No. Colly hoisted the soldiers here in a Lanky.'

'Oh,' said Biggles.

The different parties on the oasis now began to sort themselves out. Naturally, the Europeans drifted together. The Askaris began forthwith to clear the mines away from the water-hole. The Touregs watched for a time, and then silently faded away into the desert that was their home, heading in single file towards the setting sun. Biggles had told the sheikh that in a few days the oasis would be safe.

Explanations followed. Biggles narrated briefly what had happened on the oasis, and Bertie, at greater length, told of his flight to Khartoum, and of his meeting there with Wilks.

'Bit of luck finding Wilks there,' observed Biggles. 'He's a good scout. I think you did quite right to follow the Renkells. What I'm most pleased about is your getting their compass course. If we follow that line it ought to take us to Gontermann's base camp—that is, if he wasn't laying a false trail, which in the circumstances seems unlikely. My map was burnt in the Mosquito, or I'd plot the course right away to see where it leads.' He turned to Collingwood. 'How long have you been in Upper Egypt?'

'Six months.'

'Ever hear of a place called Sanseviera?'

Colly shook his head. 'Never—and I know most of the country round Khartoum. Of course, I haven't been any great distance to the east, because we don't patrol over Abyssinia.*'

Biggles started. 'Abyssinia! Of course! By thunder!— that's the answer. Scaroni served in Abyssinia during the campaign. He probably knows every inch of the country. Abyssinia would be a central point for striking at the Persian Gulf, Kenya, and the Mediterranean. Scaroni had got another of his secret dumps there— buried the stuff, no doubt, to prevent it from falling into our hands when we pushed the Italians out. We'll get along to Khartoum right away, and take up the trail again from there. Are you going to stay here with the Askaris, Collingwood?'

'No, my orders are to leave them here to clean up, and collect them in a day or two. I'm going back to Khartoum. There's plenty of room for everybody in my Lankey.'

'Any objection to starting right away?'

Colly smiled. 'I'd rather do that than sweat across this blistering desert tomorrow morning in the sun.'

'That's fine,' declared Biggles. 'Let's get cracking. Bertie, you must be tired; you go in the Lanky and snatch a snooze. Algy, you'd better go with him. Ginger can come with me in the Spur.'

And so it was decided. Biggles made a tour with

*Now Ethiopia.

Sergeant Mahmud to show him the approximate position of the mines, and then, rejoining the others, they all walked up the *wadi* to the aircraft, which had been left some distance out, Bertie having landed at the spot from which he had taken off, and followed the instructions contained in the note, which he had found. Darkness was settling over the wilderness, so without further discussion they disposed themselves as arranged. The two machines then took off and set a course for Khartoum.

The flight was uneventful, and it was just eleven o'clock when they arrived over the aerodrome and received permission to land.

In a few minutes, at Station Headquarters, Biggles was shaking hands with Wilks. Algy and Ginger took part in the reunion, for they, too, knew the Group Captain, although he had not reached that high rank when they last saw him. Wilks had been expecting them and a late supper had been laid in the mess. While this was being enjoyed, and over the coffee that followed, Biggles took his old comrade into his full confidence. This was necessary, if only because his close co-operation would be required if the pursuit of the bandits was to be pushed on without loss of time.

'I heard about the affair of the *Calpurnia*,' said Wilks, when Biggles had finished. 'In fact, Egypt is buzzing with it. They say there's an unholy row over the loss of the rajah's jewels.'

'So I imagine,' returned Biggles. 'I shall have to get in touch with the Yard right away to let Raymond know that we're doing something about it. He hasn't the remotest idea of where we are or what we're doing. I'll bet he's tearing his hair out in handfuls. That isn't our fault; things have happened too fast for me to keep him informed. I doubt if even he realised that this chase was going to take us half-way across the world. What are the chances of getting a cable through from here?'

'You can send a cable in the ordinary way from the post office,' answered Wilks. 'But as this is something of a national matter, and confidential, I feel justified in sending a signal through, in code, to the Air Ministry, who will pass it on to Raymond.'

'That's fine,' asserted Biggles. 'The difficulty is to know how much to tell him. I think, as matters stand, all we can say is that we're on the track, and expect results shortly. Another thing I must do is get a spare machine, a Mosquito if possible, from the aircraft park at Heliopolis. They have some there. If they say I can have one, perhaps you wouldn't mind one of your lads flying Algy and Bertie up to fetch it?'

'Not in the least,' agreed Wilks. 'But do you really expect results?'

'It all depends on how my two clues pan out,' replied Biggles. 'The first is the compass course on which the Renkells were flying. That should give us the general line. We can plot it in the map room. The other is a place called Sanseviera—or something like that; Grindler happened to mention it in the course of conversation. By rights, it should be on the course the bandits were flying. Did you ever hear of a place of that name?'

Wilks shook his head. 'Never—although there's plenty of it not far from here. There's a lot in the Sudd—you know, the swamp higher up the river.'

Biggles looked puzzled. 'I don't understand. A lot of what?'

'Sanseviera.'

Biggles started. 'What the devil are you talking about?'

'I'm talking about sanseviera.'

'Listen, old boy,' murmured Biggles, 'I'm trying to remain calm. Will you please tell me, in plain, simple English, what is this sanseviera?'

'I mean the stuff that grows.'

'*Grows?*'

'Yes, it's a plant.'

Understanding dawned in Biggles's eyes. 'Good Lord!' he breathed.

'Didn't you know?' inquired Wilks.

'What gave you the idea that I was a professor of botany?' demanded Biggles. 'Horticulture isn't my long suit. Tell me more about this stuff.'

'Frankly, I don't know much about it myself, except that it's something to avoid,' answered Wilks. 'The common name is bow-string hemp. It's a tall, spiny bush, rather like a cactus. I believe there are different sorts, but the stuff around here sprouts up a bunch of leaves that look like flattish cylinders, mottled, about six feet high. You find it all over East Africa. In fact, I hear they are cultivating it now in Kenya—they make ropes out of the fibres. There's a whole forest of it, hundreds of square miles, just over the frontier in Abyssinia. I happen to know that because during the war, on a reconnaissance, one of my lads, a chap named Saunders, made a forced landing in the blasted stuff. It took him a fortnight to find a way out. He reckoned he never would have got out had he not been found by some Samburus—the local people. Saunders told me that the place was mostly swamp, crawling with croco-

167

diles, snakes, and bugs of all shapes and sizes. He was nearly torn to pieces by mosquitoes.'

During this recital Biggles sat staring at Wilks's face. 'Well, I'm dashed! So *that's* it?' he muttered at the finish. 'What a set-up. I should never have guessed. Now we're getting somewhere. It looks as if Gontermann's permanent hide-out is somewhere in that cactus patch.'

'If it is, you're going to have a lovely time trying to find it,' opined Wilks.

'If the compass course crosses it, and I'm willing to bet my brolly that it does, by following the line we ought to hit the camp.'

'That may be so,' agreed Wilks. 'And then what?'

'I see what you mean,' said Biggles slowly. 'If we fly over it we shall be seen, and if we are seen the blighters will know we're on their track.'

'Exactly. How are you going to get at them?'

'How about dropping a bomb or two on them, to stir them up—if you see what I mean?' suggested Bertie. 'Scatter them, and all that.'

'A direct hit would also scatter the rajah's jewels,' Biggles pointed out. 'Apart from that, we're policemen now, not war flyers, and a policeman isn't justified in dishing out his own idea of justice even though he may shoot in self-defence. I aim to catch this skunk Gontermann, and deliver him, alive, to those who will see that he answers for his crimes with a nice piece of new rope round his neck. Shooting is too good for him.' Biggles turned back to Wilks. 'All the same, remind me to borrow a gun from you—in case. I wonder if we could get into this sanseviera stuff on foot?'

'I should be sorry to try that,' declared Wilks. 'Abyssinia is wild country, and since the people were sprayed with poison gas by the Italians they take a pretty dim view of white men, regardless of nationality.'

'But Gontermann and Co. are there,' argued Biggles.

'They probably keep the locals at a distance with machine-guns,' returned Wilks. 'You couldn't play that sort of game. Another point you appear to have overlooked is, you'd have to get permission to fly over Abyssinia. People are getting particular as to who waffles about over their territory.'

'Who's going to stop us?'

'The Abyssinian Air Force might—the Emperor* has one, you know, at Addis Ababa. If you start scrapping with them you'd be liable to start another war. This is really a matter for the Foreign Office.'

'I'm afraid you're right,' agreed Biggles. 'We don't want to start another rumpus. I'll tell Raymond that we've located the crooks in Western Abyssinia, and ask him to get permission for us to go in from the Abyssinian Minister in London. That would keep us safe from the political angle.'

'Whatever you do, you'll always be faced with the difficulty of making an air reconnaissance without being seen, and once you're spotted you'll be handicapped from the start,' said Wilks pensively. 'I don't see how you can get over that.'

'There's always a way of getting over an obstacle— if you can find it,' remarked Biggles. 'That's one of my little axioms.' A twinkle came into his eyes. 'I think I've got it. You say Abyssinia has its own air force?'

'Yes.'

*Haile Selassie, Emperor of Abyssinia between 1930–1974.

'What machines do they use?'

'I'm not sure about that,' answered Wilks. 'We had a formation over here a week or two back on a courtesy visit; but they were trainers—Tiger Moths.'

'Have you got any Tiger Moths here?'

'Yes, we've a couple. We use them for co-operation with the Askaris.' Wilks looked suspicious. 'What's the bright idea?'

'From what you tell me,' explained Biggles, 'it wouldn't be a remarkable thing if an Abyssinian Tiger Moth flew across this sanseviera area. I mean, Gontermann wouldn't take any notice of that.'

Wilks looked puzzled. 'I don't get it. We haven't got an Abyssinian Tiger Moth, and if you're thinking of going to Addis Ababa to borrow one you'll have grey hair before you get back. Our Tigers wear R.A.F ring markings.'

Biggles grinned. 'Did you never hear of a stuff called paint? They say you can't make a leopard change his spots, but we could make one of your Tigers change his stripes by painting out our own nationality marks and substituting those of the venerable land of Ethiopia.'

'Hey! Wait a minute,' cried Wilks. 'Do you want to get me court-martialled?'

'Frankly, I don't care what you get, old bloodhound, as long as I get these infernal crooks,' returned Biggles lightly.

'You always were a calculating son-of-a-gun,' growled Wilks. But humour glinted in his eyes. 'All right. I'll do it. All the same, you owe it to the Foreign Office to let them know that you propose to cruise over a prohibited area, in case you run into trouble or have a forced landing.'

'Now you're talking,' declared Biggles. He grinned again. 'No use having pals if you don't use them sometimes.'

'You write out your message for Raymond and I'll see that it's transmitted by radio right away,' invited Wilks. 'Then, if you don't mind, I'll get some sleep. I've work to do tomorrow.'

'Now you remind me, I could do with a spot of shut-eye myself,' said Biggles, yawning.

Chapter 15

The Sanseviera

The air police were at breakfast the following morning when the answer to Biggles's signal to Air Commodore Raymond was received. Wilks brought it into the mess, and delivered it personally. He was smiling.

'I should say your remark about Raymond tearing his hair out was understatement rather than exaggeration,' he observed. 'Here's your answer—I've had it decoded.'

'Read it,' requested Biggles, reaching for the coffee.

Wilks's smile broadened as he read:

'Owing to Calpurnia *affair matter has become a political issue in Parliament stop I shall be on the mat unless you end racket stop Go where you like and do what you like as long as you get crooks stop Leave subsequent explanations to me stop R.A.F., Middle East Command, has been ordered by Secretary of State for Air to co-operate without limit stop Signed Raymond.'*

A smile spread slowly over Biggles's face. 'Strewth! Raymond must be in a sweat to send a message like that. I like the last part—that relieves you of any responsibility, Wilks.'

Wilks folded the message. 'It looks as if you'd better get cracking, my merry sleuths,' he advised.

'You can get *your* boys cracking with their paint pots,

on a Tiger Moth, for a start,' requested Biggles. 'I'm
going to cast an eye over this sanseviera jungle.'

'They're already on the job,' answered Wilks.

'Good. In that case you can go and ring up Heliopolis
to see if I can borrow a Mosquito.'

'It's done,' announced Wilks. 'The machine is on
the tarmac waiting for someone to fetch it. Collingwood
is standing by to fly Algy and Bertie up, as soon as
they've finished wolfing my last pot of marmalade.'

Biggles chuckled. 'You always were one for keeping
pace with things. Get moving, Algy, and make it
snappy.'

'What do we do when we've got the Mosquito?'
asked Algy, rising, with a piece of toast still in his
hand.

'Bring it here—that's all for the time being. I'll take
Ginger with me on this jungle jaunt; we ought to be
back before you are. What we do after that will depend
on what we find. We can't do anything until we locate
Gontermann's hide-out.'

'Okay,' said Algy. With a wave Bertie followed him
to the door.

Biggles also rose, and tossed his napkin on the table.
'Come on, Ginger, if you want to sit in my spare seat.
I'm all agog to run an optic over this botanical bunk-
hole.'

'Anything more I can do?' asked Wilks.

'Yes, you can get me a nice big automatic and a
couple of spare clips of slugs,' answered Biggles. 'I'd
better have a pocket compass, too.' He went out to
the aerodrome where a placid-looking Tiger Moth was
receiving the final touches of its transfiguration.

In ten minutes, while the paint was still tacky,

Biggles was in the air, flying south-east on the compass course that Bertie had given him, towards the Abyssinian border. This was well over two hundred miles distant, or a two hours' flight each way, and as the Tiger, even with a special long-range tank, had an endurance of just over five hours, it left only an hour—allowing a margin of safety—for the actual reconnaissance. Fortunately, the sanseviera area began not far from the border.

When this was reached, the country below, while bearing no resemblance to the desert, was nearly as depressing. The tangled mass of undergrowth, which Biggles knew must be the sanseviera, occurred first in scattered outposts; but these soon became larger, and eventually merged into one vast, dull green panorama, stretching as far as the eye could see, undulating rather than flat, with outcrops of gaunt rock sometimes breaking through the higher parts. There were numerous pools of water, frequently linked together by winding channels, and an occasional open space, or group of flat-topped trees, caused presumably by a change in the nature of the soil. If there were any paths through this hideous blemish on the earth's surface, they could not be seen. Yet, as Biggles pointed out, it was fairly certain that there must be paths, for twice he went low to examine the source of smoke which curled upward, and on each occasion it came from a small village.

Biggles surveyed the gloomy picture with disfavour. 'What a place—what a mess,' he muttered. 'Fancy getting lost in that lot.'

Sometimes circling over suspicious-looking areas, but always returning to the original compass course, Biggles went on, and at the end, after covering nearly seventy miles of it, came to the far side of the sanseviera jungle. The growth gave way to arid, rocky hills. By that time he was near the limit of his petrol range, so, without finding what he sought, he was compelled to fly straight back to the aerodrome. He made no secret of his disappointment.

Bertie and Algy were not yet back, but they landed some time later in the new Mosquito.

The same afternoon Biggles made another five-hour reconnaissance, again without result. He went out the following morning as soon as it was light, and returned, disgruntled, to report no progress. Algy and Bertie went out, using the same Tiger Moth. They, too, came back depressed, with nothing to report.

'I know what the trouble is,' said Biggles savagely, as they dressed on the third morning. 'They've got the place camouflaged—too well camouflaged. But there, I suppose that was only to be expected. No doubt they all know something about camouflage, but Scaroni, as a transport and supply officer, is probably an expert. I'm sick of flying up and down over the cursed stuff, but there's nothing else for it. What worries me is, if we go on like this Gontermann will realise that the Tiger isn't just a casual machine passing over; not being a fool he'll know that somebody is looking for him. Come on, Ginger, let's have another shot.'

The Tiger went off. Collingwood also went off, to Zufra, and returned later with the Askaris, who had finished their job of mine clearing. Biggles wasn't interested in mines, or Zufra. The reconnaissance had revealed nothing, and he was getting desperate. His state of mind was not improved when a signal was received from Raymond, demanding in no uncertain terms to be informed what he thought he was doing.

Biggles looked at the others, with eyes weary and bloodshot from long hours in the air. 'He wants to know what we are doing,' he said plaintively. 'I don't know what to tell him, and that's a fact.'

'You can tell him we're all going nuts, looking for a needle in a haystack a hundred miles square,' muttered Algy.

Wilks was sympathetic, but had no suggestion to make.

Biggles turned towards the mess. 'Let's have some lunch. I'll try again this afternoon.'

Half an hour later, surprisingly, another signal was received from Raymond. This time it contained information, and Biggles whistled joyfully when he read it. 'Listen,' he said. 'I'd completely forgotten that I'd asked the B.B.C. to listen for signals. Raymond says they've picked up something; they can't decipher it; all they can say is, something is coming over the air from an unknown source in Africa. They've sent us the bearing, in case it is any help to us.'

'Is it?' asked Bertie, vaguely.

'I'll say it is!' cried Biggles. 'That is, if it is Gontermann signalling to Preuss, as I hope. It's the answer to my prayer.'

'How do you work that out?' asked Algy.

'Because, if we strike this bearing from London across Africa, and then plot the course the Renkells took from Zufra, the point where the two lines meet—if they do—will be the place we're looking for. Let's go to the map room.'

After a few busy minutes with a pencil and ruler

Biggles let out a cry of triumph. 'We've got it!' he declared, stabbing the map with the point of his pencil.

His enthusiasm was not without justification, for the two lines he had drawn cut across each other in the middle of the sanseviera.

'And now what are you going to do?' asked Wilks dispassionately. 'You must have flown over that spot before. If you fly over it again it's ten to one you'll still see nothing.'

'I'm not going to fly over it,' asserted Biggles grimly. 'I'm going to land.'

'In the sanseviera?' cried Wilks, aghast.

'In the nearest clearing that I can find to this spot.'

'You're crazy.'

'Maybe; but I shall soon go crazy, anyway, if I go on flying over that perishing jungle.'

'And suppose Gontermann and his gang *are* there?' inquired Wilks. 'What are two of you going to do against that bunch?'

'There'll be four of us,' retorted Biggles. 'We'll borrow the other Tiger.'

'And what if you bust them trying to get down?'

'If we make crash landings we'll clear a proper runway, so that you can fetch us out with a Lanky.'

'Suffering Icarus!' cried Wilks. 'What do you think this is—a circus? By the time you've finished you'll have my machines scattered half-way across the blinking continent.'

'That'll give you something to do—picking 'em up,' persisted Biggles. 'Come on, don't stand there blowing through your whiskers. Trot out that spare Tiger. Never mind about painting fresh colours on it—I'm in a hurry.'

'It's taken me twenty years to climb to Group Captain,' muttered Wilks in a resigned voice. 'By the time you've finished running my station I shall be back to aircraftman, second class.'

'Then you can start to climb up again,' said Biggles, grinning. 'Now you've had some practice you ought to be able to do it in nineteen years. Come on, chaps, let's get cracking. Algy, you follow in the second machine. If I can find a clearing without too many obstructions I'll go down first; if it's okay for you to follow I'll give you a wave.'

'Good enough,' agreed Algy cheerfully. 'Thank goodness things are looking up at last.'

'You'll probably change your mind about that when you've trodden on a snake or two, or tripped over a crocodile,' growled Wilks.

'Don't take any notice of him,' scoffed Biggles. 'He always was a pessimistic cove.'

Wilks's sunburned face flashed a smile. Then he became serious. 'Will you take a tip from me?'

Biggles noticed the change in his manner. 'I'll always take a tip from the man on the spot,' he assented.

'Take Sergeant Mahmud with you—he's back from Zufra.'

'For what purpose?'

'He may save you a packet of trouble if you encounter hostility. He speaks Amharic, the local lingo.'

'I see,' said Biggles slowly. 'It'll mean leaving one of the others behind, but I think you've got something there, Wilks. Sergeant Mahmud will fly with Algy. Sorry, Bertie, old boy, but you'll have to stand down. Wilks is right; it's in the best interests of the expedition.'

Bertie's face fell, but he was too well disciplined to argue. 'Pity, and all that,' he sighed. 'Isn't there something else I can do?'

'Yes, as a matter of fact, there is,' returned Biggles. 'We should look silly, shouldn't we, if one of the Renkells—or both of them for that matter—decided to pull out, leaving us staggering about in a couple of Tigers. You take the Spur and patrol the frontier. Keep high and you'll be able to watch a lot of sky. Should one of the Renkells try to break out, go for him.'

Bertie polished his eyeglass without enthusiasm. 'As you say, noble chief. Since birth it has been my fate to hold the dud end of the stick.'

'You never know which is the dud end until afterwards. You may have all the luck,' predicted Biggles, with unsuspected accuracy as it turned out. 'Well, we'll push along. Cheerio, Wilks. See you later.'

'You hope,' murmured Wilks.

In a few minutes the two Tigers were in the air, Biggles and Ginger in one, and Algy, with Sergeant Mahmud as passenger, in the other.

In spite of his inconsequential manner Biggles was under no delusion as to the dangerous nature of the task in front of him. The landing in the sanseviera, a hazardous expedient, was only the beginning. After that there would be the bandits, and that they would fight with all the weapons they possessed was not to be doubted. By this time he knew the general configuration of the country, and such landmarks as there were; and although he made straight for the pin-point indicated by the crossed lines on his map, he had no intention of flying over it, knowing that if he did he must inevitably be seen by the bandits, who, if not actually

179

suspicious of this prowling Tiger Moth, would be on the alert. He wanted, if possible, to take them by surprise. He hoped to find a landing-ground, one of the several comparatively open areas in the sanseviera, a few miles short of his objective—not too close, in case they should be heard. He recalled that there were some, but he did not know which was the best for his purpose, for he had never examined them with this object in view.

He circled low over half a dozen before he made his choice. The first four were too small, or too narrow, and the fifth had a village in the middle of it. The sixth, which he reckoned to be about five miles from the pin-point, was the best, so far. It was by no means an ideal landing-ground, and would have been out of the question for a heavy machine, being narrow, slightly on the slope, with a rough surface; but he thought it unlikely that he would find anything better, so he decided to take a chance.

The aircraft bumped and rocked when he put it down, and all but turned over when a wheel encountered a low bush; but it finished on even keel, so he taxied on to leave a clear run in for the following machine. Before signalling to Algy to land he went out and tore up the bush that had nearly turned him over. A quick survey of the clearing also enabled him to indicate the best area. With this advantage Algy landed without mishap. Both machines were now put in position for a quick take-off should one become necessary, after which Biggles produced the compass, without which progress on foot through the jungle would have been sheer guesswork.

The value of Wilks's tip was at once proved, for there

now appeared from the jungle a figure dressed in half-African, half-European style. That is to say, he wore a *shamma*, which looked like a piece of sheet, wrapped round his body, and over it, incongruously, a Sam Browne belt. A dilapidated slough hat, much too large, that had once obviously been the property of an Australian soldier, covered his head. In his left hand he carried a long spear, the butt of which rested on the ground, so that he was able to use the shaft as a support for his left leg, which in some curious way appeared to be curled round it. The impression created was of a one-legged man. A rifle sloped across his right shoulder.

'A Danakil,' said Sergeant Mahmud, and called to the man in what, presumably, was his own language.

A brief long-distance exchange of words followed. At the end the man advanced, reluctantly, and Sergeant Mahmud, acting as interrogator and interpreter, extracted this information. The local man, as he had already conjectured from his habit of standing on one leg, was of the Danakil tribe. His name was Burradidi, and he was a hunter by profession. He was then out on a hunting trip. In answer to a question as to whether there were any white men in the vicinity, he answered emphatically that there were, at the same time pointing the direction with his spear. It was on this account that he had been nervous about coming forward, for until Sergeant Mahmud had declared himself to be a British soldier he had feared that the newcomers might be friends of these same white men. Asked if he would guide the party to these other white men, Burradidi refused point-blank, declaring that this was impossible. No one would go within miles of the place on account of the 'air that killed.' This 'air that killed' puzzled

Biggles for some moments, until he realised that the man was talking about poison gas.

'Gontermann mentioned to me that Scaroni had provided them with other weapons besides mines,' he said in a hard voice. 'Poison gas bombs must be one of them. That, apparently, is how they keep the locals at a distance. The more I learn about these thugs and their methods the more delighted I shall be to see them strung up.' To Sergeant Mahmud he said, 'Explain to this chap that we have come to capture these users of air that kills. If he will help us to do this, the country will be well rid of them, and he shall have a hundred dollars* into the bargain.'

At first the Danakil demurred, but a hundred dollars was a big sum of money, and in the end avarice gained ascendancy over fear. He offered to show them a path by which the camp could be reached; he would go part, but not all the way.

This suited Biggles, who, as a preliminary measure, merely wanted to find out the exact location of the bandits' base, and ascertain how the flying part of it was organised—why it was, for instance, that no landing-ground was visible from the air.

The Danakil struck off into the jungle on a course that tallied with the pin-point, much to Biggles's satisfaction. For the first time he was able to appreciate all that Wilks had said about the sanseviera. Burradidi had mentioned a path, but knowing the usual African idea of a path Biggles was astonished to find a passage

*The only coins acceptable to natives of Abyssinia were Maria Theresa dollars, which had been the common currency for many years. They are now obsolete.

more in the nature of a road. There was no surface to it, but swampy areas were made passable by 'corduroy' tracks of tree-trunks lain side by side. The ugly sanseviera had encroached, and in places almost met overhead, which accounted for the fact that the road could not be seen from the air.

'I don't understand this,' remarked Biggles. 'This isn't a natural path. It looks more like an abandoned military road. By thunder! I've got it. Of course—what a fool I am. The Italians must have made this track during or after their conquest of the country, when they were trying to subdue the outlying tribes.'

Sergeant Mahmud questioned the Danakil on this point, and found that this was the case.

'It's Zufra all over again,' declared Biggles. 'Scaroni was with the Italians, and used this track for the transport of stores and petrol. No doubt he told Baumer about it. It wouldn't surprise me if we found a serviceable landing-ground, suitable for military aircraft, at the end. No wonder our fellows never found the petrol dump. Scaroni wouldn't have to go to much trouble to hide it, in this stuff.' He glanced at the scene around them.

It was all that Wilks's informant, the pilot Saunders, had said of it—and more. The ground was little better than a swamp—enormous tussocks of coarse grass with pools of black, stagnant, evil-looking water, between them. From the tussocks sprang the coarse, mottled leaves, or rather spines, of the prevailing sanseviera. Rustlings in the grass, and soft furtive plops in the water, suggested a wealth of reptile life. Enormous black flies, as well as mosquitoes, rose in the clouds. The air was hot, humid, and heavy with the stench of rotting vegetation. The travellers sweated copiously as they marched, striking at the flies that swarmed about them, and tried to settle in their eyes. The great wonder to Ginger was how Saunders had managed to live for a fortnight in such horror without going mad.

For about an hour the party went forward through a never-changing scene. Then the Danakil stopped, and pointed with his spear. He would go no farther.

Biggles took the lead. 'Come on,' he said softly. 'No more talking.'

Chapter 16
The Poison Belt

Almost imperceptibly the scene began to change. The vivid green of the jungle turned slowly to a rusty yellow. The sanseviera still reared its octopus-like arms, but they were dead, and remembering what the Danakil had said it did not take Biggles long to guess the reason.

'Poison gas did that,' he whispered. 'If Gontermann has used it against the Abyssinians he won't hesitate to use it against us. Quietly now.'

They moved forward, slowly, picking their way with care, and in this manner reached the outer fringe of the enemy camp. By that time they were all gasping for breath, and Biggles understood why Grindler had prefixed the word sanseviera with a curse. There was something about the steaming atmosphere that was not only oppressive, but positively suffocating. The place stank with the acrid smell of vegetation that had grown and died and rotted in successive layers through centuries of time. An occasional skeleton lying in the tangle of undergrowth did nothing to enliven the scene.

'Probably Abyssinians who were gassed,' said Biggles, referring to them, as he paused to wipe the sweat from his face.

It was at this stage that Algy made a remark which was to have far-reaching results, although he was unaware of it. Sergeant Mahmud was quietly preparing for action, and in the course of this he took from his

185

pocket a pair of hand grenades and hung them on his belt. Algy looked at them with a disapproval which he made no attempt to hide.

'Look what the sergeant's produced,' he growled. 'He wouldn't have flown in my machine with those in his pocket if I'd known about it.'

'Very good,' said Sergeant Mahmud, imperturbably, tapping a grenade.

Biggles turned to look. 'You be careful what you're doing with those things, Sergeant,' he warned.

'Very good, sir,' acknowledged the sergeant, who was a man of few words.

There was not a soul in sight; all was silent except for the constant buzz of the flies, so with the others following Biggles now made a cautious reconnaissance. It occupied some time, but by the end he had grasped the general lay-out of the place, which was so plain for all to see that it hardly called for comment. It confirmed his conjecture that the camp had been originally a war-time emergency landing-ground. Skilfully designed by army engineers, particular care had been taken against aerial observation, and it was now easy enough to understand why the flights had failed to reveal it.

There was no exposed runway. A central building of wood frame construction, loop-holed* for defence and thatched with layers of sanseviera, formed, as it were, the hub of a wheel; from it, like spokes, aisles had been cut in the jungle towards the four cardinal points of the compass. Over these aisles, camouflage netting, threaded with the eternal sanseviera, had been spread

---

*A loop hole is a small gap to fire a gun through, but not large enough for someone outside easily to fire into it.

in such a way that they could be drawn aside to permit air operations on a small scale. It was really quite simple, yet effective, even though the camouflage, bone dry and withered from long exposure to the sun, showed signs of falling to pieces. This also applied to the central hutment which, from the cover of the jungle, Biggles surveyed from a distance of about fifty yards. He could get no closer without exposing himself, for the intervening space was open, in the manner of a parade ground, although even this had been strewn with dry branches of sanseviera to prevent detection from the air.

'Well, this is it,' said Biggles quietly. 'I should say the part of the hut we're looking at is the living accommodation; the machines are probably parked under that big awning carried out on poles from the far side.'

'Just what are you aiming to do?' asked Algy.

'I want to catch these criminals alive, arrest them in the regulation manner, if possible,' replied Biggles. 'The place seems so quiet that I feel inclined to try to take it at a rush, before Gontermann can organise a defence.'

'If we could put the machine out of action for a start we should definitely make an end of their pirate pranks, whatever else happened,' suggested Ginger. 'That would fix them in this area, and put a stop to this gallivanting round the globe.'

'I think there's something in that idea,' assented Biggles. 'If I could get across to the hut without being spotted I could work my way round it to the awning. We've got to cross the open, anyway, to reach the place. No doubt it was to prevent a surprise attack that the jungle was cleared. I'll try it. You fellows stay here and keep me covered in case I bump into opposition.'

He had taken the first step into the open, and was crouching for a dash across, when an unexpected factor altered the entire situation. Round the end of the building came a gaunt, mangy, Alsatian dog. It moved quietly, as though prowling with no particular object. Biggles froze. The dog stopped abruptly. Its nose went up, feeling the air, as though it had caught a suspicious taint. Its head came round and it looked straight at Biggles. It stiffened and bared its teeth, growling deep in its throat; then it broke into a clamour of furious barking which was all the more devastating on account of the previous silence. Inside the hut somebody shouted. Feet thudded on bare boards.

Seeing that it was now impossible to proceed with his plan, Biggles backed hastily into cover, and with a crisp, 'Come on,' to the others, started to work his way round the clearing, away from the point where the animal had located them. He had no fixed plan. Indeed, in his heart he knew that now the alarm had been raised the odds were all against them, but he still hoped that it might be possible to reach the Renkills and put them out of service. This hope was short-lived. The dog followed, barking, and to complete the pandemonium a machine-gun came into action. A burst of bullets raked the spot they had just vacated.

Biggles blundered on, heedless of thorns and spines that tore at his clothes; but he pulled up short when a metal object, about the size of a cricket ball, came bounding across the clearing. It exploded with a sullen bang, splashing in all directions a black, oily fluid, from which vapour drifted sluggishly.

'The air that kills. No good,' muttered Sergeant Mahmud.

'Mustard gas,*' rasped Biggles, as another gas bomb exploded. 'I can't see where the infernal things are coming from. It's no use, chaps. We can't fight that stuff. Let's get out of this before we're skinned alive. Back to the path!' His face was pale with chagrin.

They had started to retire when, as if he had suddenly remembered something, he caught the sergeant by the shoulder. 'Just a minute, Sergeant,' he said tersely. 'I hate letting them have things *all* their own way. Give me those grenades.'

Sergeant Mahmud handed them over. 'Very good,' said he.

Biggles's face was set in grim lines as he forced a way to the edge of the clearing, where he crouched for a moment while he tore the safety-pins from the grenades with his teeth. Then he made a short rush and flung the missiles in quick succession. The first landed on the roof of the hut; the second struck the side of the awning and dropped among the debris at the bottom. The two explosions merged. He did not wait for the smoke to clear to observe results, as the enemy continued to fire blindly through the smoke and the bullets were coming dangerously close. Moreover, another gas bomb came lobbing across the clearing. He dashed back to where the others were waiting, and shouting,

---

*Highly poisonous substance, odourless and virtually colourless, it causes severe burning to the skin, and lungs.

'Run for it!' plunged on towards the path by which they had approached.

'That confounded dog upset the apple-cart,' he panted, as he ran on. Shots were still being fired from the hut, and the bullets came slashing through the mushy sanseviera. Not until they were some distance down the path did he ease the pace.

'I imagine this is what the papers call being repulsed in confusion,' grunted Ginger.

'Not having respirators* or gas-proof equipment there was no sense in staying where we were,' returned Biggles. 'Once we were discovered it was all up. We couldn't see them, but they could evidently see us.' Biggles went on at a steady dog-trot.

'What are we going to do?' asked Algy.

'Get back to Khartoum as fast as we can,' replied Biggles. 'We'll come back with the Mosquito and the Spur and prang this place off the map. The rajah's sparklers will have to take their luck.'

'Look!' cried Ginger, pointing.

All eyes were turned behind and upward, to where a column of smoke was rising in the air.

'By gosh! It looks as though something has set fire to the sanseviera—perhaps the camouflage,' exclaimed Biggles. 'It must have been one of the grenades. Come to think of it, that stuff was like tinder. It should make the place easy to find when we come back. Let's keep going.'

They ran on. Ginger had never plumbed the extent of Biggles's endurance; nor did he now, although he

*A filtering system worn on the face to prevent the inhalation of poisonous gas.

ran until his heart pounded in his ears and his knees felt like jelly. Towards the finish, the journey to where the Tigers had been left became a nightmare of mud, and sweat, and flies—and sanseviera.

Not until they reached the machines did Biggles stop and look back. The pillar of smoke had become a mighty cloud that rolled up and up towards the blue dome of heaven.

'It looks as if we've given them something to think about, something to keep them busy, anyway,' he muttered.

'I should say we've done more than that,' declared Algy, still staring at the signs of a considerable conflagration. 'They may be smoked out.'

'The fire may reach their petrol,' puffed Ginger.

'Wishful thinking won't get us anywhere,' contended Biggles. 'Let's get home and fetch a load of high explosive—something to *really* warm their hides.'

Both machines took off without mishap, and flying low for maximum speed set a course for the aerodrome. From time to time Ginger looked back to note the progress of the smoke, and was pleased to see that the volume was increasing rather than diminishing. He passed this information on to Biggles, observing that Algy's prediction about the enemy being smoked out was now a real possibility.

They had just crossed the frontier, where the jungle gave way to typical Sudan desert, when Ginger, who again happened to glance back, let out a cry so shrill with alarm that Biggles turned sharply to see what was amiss.

'The Renkells!' shouted Ginger. 'They're coming this way—both of them.'

Biggles raced on. It now seemed certain that the enemy had been smoked out, or driven out by the fire—not that it mattered which—and he was by no means pleased. This evacuation was premature, and altered his plan. While the enemy were in the sanseviera he did at least know where they were, but now they might be going anywhere. It looked as if they might escape, after all, for his aircraft was neither equipped to catch the Renkells, or stop them. There were no guns in the Tiger Moths, and the comparative speeds were as a hen and a hawk. This irritating handicap so occupied his mind that it never struck him seriously that the Renkells might attack. If he thought about the possibility at all it was in an abstract sort of way; he assumed, rather, that even if the two Moths were seen, which was by no means certain, the gang would be in too much of a hurry to bother about them.

The first warning of peril came from Ginger, who suddenly shouted, 'Look out!' and Biggles, looking over his shoulder, saw the Renkells coming down like eagles on a pair of lost lambs. Their intention was instantly apparent, and after making sure that Algy was aware of the danger he prepared to take evading action, which was all he could do. Even so, he did not think much of his chance. The Tiger Moths were so far below the Renkells in speed and manoeuvrability that they would be easy marks for beginners; the enemy pilots, far from that, were experienced men of war. All he could do was skim the desert sand, keeping one eye on the enemy, nerves and muscles braced to move like lightning the instant their guns flashed.

He noted that the Wolf had picked him out, and from his own experience he could judge when the pilot would fire. At that moment he turned at right angles, so that the bullets flashed past his wing-tip to plough up the sand, and a split second later the Wolf had to zoom sharply to avoid hitting the ground. It was rather like a greyhound snatching at a hare, and just missing it on the turn.

This happened three times, and each time Biggles got away with his trick; but he did not deceive himself; he knew that it could not go on. Now that his tactics were revealed, the pilot of the Wolf would presently forestall him. Still watching his opponent, he had braced himself for the next move in the grim game of aerial 'tag', when Ginger let out a yell, shrill with excitement.

'Bertie! It's Bertie! Good old Bertie!' he shouted delightedly.

Biggles dare not take his eyes from the Wolf. He hoped, without much confidence, that the pilot would not see the Spur; but he was not surprised when the Wolf swept up in a beautiful climbing turn, no longer the attacker, but the attacked. The Spur flashed into view, coming down like a winged torpedo.

Now, for the first time in his life, Biggles had the doubtful pleasure of watching a dog-fight* from the air without taking part in it. Indeed, having no petrol to spare, he resumed his course for the aerodrome, whilst Algy, who had managed to dodge the transport, took up a position near his wing-tip.

At first Biggles was rather worried on Bertie's account, for he had two opponents, either one of which, considered on performance, would have been a fair

*An aerial battle rather than a hit-and-run attack.

match; and the transport had turned, as if the pilot intended to make the duel between the Spur and the Wolf a three-cornered combat. But then, to Biggles's utter amazement, it suddenly straightened out, turned, and sped away across the desert, the pilot clearly having decided to save his machine while its consort engaged the Spur.

'Did you see that?' cried Ginger. 'The transport's packed up. What a pal! What a pal! I wonder who's flying it?'

Biggles was wondering the same thing, but he felt pretty certain that Gontermann was in the escaping machine, probably with his friend Baumer.

The combat between the Spur and the Wolf did not last long. As far as the machines were concerned, odds were about even, but Bertie, without indulging in any wild aerobatics, out-manœuvred his opponent. In fact, he only fired twice, each time from short range, whereas the pilot of the Wolf revealed anxiety by shooting frequently from outside effective range, evidently hoping for a lucky hit—which, admittedly, happens sometimes, but not often.

The first time Bertie fired, after a clean, calculated turn, he shot a piece off the Wolf's tail unit. The Wolf flashed round in professional style and fired back, whereupon the Spur rocketed, fell off on its wing and went down in a spin. Not even Biggles knew if this was accidental or deliberate. Anyway, the Wolf followed it down, and thereby made a fatal blunder, for the Spur recovered, and coming up under its adversary raked it from nose to tail-skid.

'Got him!' yelled Ginger, in a voice hoarse with excitement.

He was right. The Wolf went on down, obviously in difficulties. Near the ground it managed to flatten out, without having lowered its wheels. It struck the desert with a crash, throwing up a cloud of dust, and rolled over and over, cart-wheeling, breaking up and flinging pieces of fabric, wood, and metal, all round the fractured fuselage.

Biggles side-slipped down to the stricken machine and landed. He jumped out, and was running over to the wreck when he saw the Spur coming down, wheels lowered, also with the obvious intention of landing. Feeling that this was an unnecessary risk he waved Bertie away; but the Spur ignored his signals and landed heavily. Biggles paid no further attention to it, but with Ginger keeping him company ran on to the Wolf. The first thing he saw was Scaroni, who had been thrown clear, with his head twisted under him at a ghastly angle.

'Poor devil,' said Biggles. 'He's got what he had coming to him. We needn't waste time there.'

Von Zoyton was the other occupant. He was still in his seat, held in place by the safety belt. His eyes were dull, but recognition gleamed in them for a moment as they fell on Biggles. His lips moved, parting in a cold, sardonic smile, and he muttered: 'If the fools hadn't left us—we could—have got you—Bigglesworth.'

'Who left you?' asked Biggles quietly, unfastening the safety belt.

'Gontermann—always for himself.'

Biggles nodded. 'Baumer was no friend of yours, or he'd have stayed.'

'He would do—what Gontermann—ordered,' was the laboured reply.

'Is Grindler with them?'

'*Ja.*'

'What about Renkell?'

Von Zoyton did not answer. He was obviously on the point of collapse, so Biggles and Ginger, between them, got the wounded man out of his seat, and into the meagre shade of a tattered wing.

'I warned you to get clear of that bunch of crooks,' said Biggles sadly.

'Your friend—flies well,' muttered von Zoyton.

Biggles smiled. 'You've met before—in the desert.

'Ah. Which one—was it?'

'Lord Lissie.'

'With the eyeglass. I remember him.'

'Why did you take off?' asked Biggles.

'Had to. You burnt—us out. I told Gontermann that stuff—was too dry . . . but he wouldn't—listen. You won't get the jewels, though, Bigglesworth. He's got them—with him.'

Biggles started. 'Where's he bound for?'

'America. *Ach!*' The German's face twisted with pain. '*Mir geht . . . nicht sehr gut,**' he gasped.

'Hang on. We'll get you to hospital,' promised Biggles. He glanced up as Algy's voice came across the silence. 'What's Algy shouting about?' he muttered.

Algy had also landed, and seeing that Bertie had not left his machine went over to congratulate him. His frantic shouts took Biggles and Ginger over at the double.

'Bertie's stopped one—in the thigh, I think,' greeted Algy urgently.

*German: I'm feeling . . . not too good.

196

Biggles climbed up to the cockpit. Bertie was still sitting in his seat. His face was ashen, but his monocle was still in his eye. He smiled weakly. 'Got my leg in the way—silly ass thing to do. Sorry—and so on.' And with that he fainted dead away.

'Let's get him out,' said Biggles curtly.

They got Bertie out of the cockpit and found an ugly wound in the upper part of his right leg. He had lost a good deal of blood, but using the bandages from the first-aid kit they managed to stop the bleeding.

'Scaroni's dead,' Biggles told Algy. 'Von Zoyton is in a bad way. I fancy he's got broken bones. I want to get on after Gontermann, but we shall have to get him to hospital as well as Bertie. I'll tell you what,' he went on, clipping his words. 'I'll fly Bertie to Khartoum in the Spur. Algy, you follow with von Zoyton. Ginger, you fly the other Tiger. Sergeant Mahmud will have to stay here to keep the hyenas away from Scaroni's body until the ambulance comes out. I shall be at Khartoum first so I'll tell Wilks what has happened. Ginger should have arrived by the time I've finished, so we'll push right on after Gontermann. You can follow in the Mosquito, Algy. You'll be last in, so I shan't wait for you; make for Zufra; failing that, Tripoli; von Zoyton says Gontermann is heading for America, but he'll have to refuel somewhere before starting across the Ditch*. From what Bertie told us there must be petrol at Zufra, so the transport may make for the oasis. I shall go there first, anyway. Let's get cracking. The transport's got ten minutes start as it is.'

*Slang: Atlantic Ocean.

They lifted Bertie into the spare seat of the Spur and made him as comfortable as possible. Von Zoyton, who had now lost consciousness was carried to Algy's Tiger. Biggles then took off in the Spur. He was followed by Ginger, flying solo. Algy, with his limp passenger, then took the air, leaving Sergeant Mahmud standing at attention by the wreck, a lonely figure in the wilderness.

Chapter 17
Gontermann Does It Again

Biggles landed at Khartoum and taxied tail-up to the tarmac where his yell brought everyone within hearing running towards the Spur, including Wilks, who was in station headquarters. Within thirty seconds the ambulance was alongside, and Bertie, now conscious, lamenting his enforced retirement from the affair, was raced away to hospital.

'I shall be back just as soon as this business sorts itself out,' Biggles promised him.

He then turned to Wilks and asked him to get the Spur refuelled in the shortest possible time. Wilks gave the order, and while mechanics were busy on the machine Biggles gave him a concise account of what had happened.

'You'd better send a vehicle out for Sergeant Mahmud,' he concluded. 'Please yourself what you do about the Wolf. Perhaps you'd better bring the pieces in—Air Ministry experts may want to look at them.'

'Pity you couldn't have got the transport at the same time,' murmured Wilks. 'It looks as if the four ring-leaders have got away after all.'

'Three of them have—so far,' replied Biggles. 'I don't know about Renkell, but I imagine he's in the party. I shall push on as soon as Ginger comes in. For your guidance, should anything go wrong, my first objective will be Zufra. If I don't catch up with them there I shall go on to Tripoli. Beyond that, I don't know.'

'The transport's got a good start; do you think you'll catch it?' asked Wilks anxiously.

'Yes, I do, because it can't get off this continent without refuelling,' answered Biggles. 'Somewhere it will have to lose the time I'm losing here. Apart from that I should say the Spur is a trifle faster than the transport. Ah! Here comes Ginger now.'

'You're not stopping for food?' queried Wilks.

'I'm not stopping for anything once Ginger's on the ground,' declared Biggles.

As soon as Ginger landed Biggles called him over and climbed back into the Spur. Algy's Tiger Moth could be seen in the distance, but Biggles did not wait for him. He took off at once and headed out over the desert on the long flight to El Zufra. Naturally, he watched the sky ahead, although he hardly expected to overtake the transport, even if he had correctly predicted its destination.

During the entire flight neither he nor Ginger saw anything except an implacable sky of lapis lazuli overhead, and the pitiless distances on all sides. The sun toiled wearily across the heavens, splashing gold with a lavish hand and striking the ground with silent force. At last the oasis crept up over the horizon, like an island in a sea that had been suddenly arrested in motion.

'Are you going to land?' asked Ginger.

'I don't know, yet,' answered Biggles as, with his eyes surveying the ground he roared low over the palms.

'They're not here,' said Ginger in a disappointed voice.

'We shall have to make sure,' replied Biggles. 'The machine may be under that awning, in which case we shouldn't be able to see it. Naturally, they'd keep out of sight when they heard us coming. I'm going down. If they're here, not knowing that the mines have been cleared, they'll expect us to land in the *wadi*, so that's where they'll have their guns trained. It should give them quite a shock to see us land on the other side without being blown up. Five minutes will be time enough to settle whether they are here or not.'

Lowering his wheels, he landed, not in the *wadi*, but on the opposite side of the oasis, allowing the machine to run on until it was near the fringe of palms.

'You stay here and look after the machine, in case of accidents,' he ordered. Leaving the engine ticking over he jumped down and walked briskly into the oasis.

As he strode on towards the depression over which the awning was spread he noticed a piece of paper in a cleft stick, erected in the manner of a notice-board, but at the moment he was too occupied with other matters to make the detour that would have been necessary to see what it was. Automatic in hand he ran up a slight eminence, the top of which he knew commanded a view of the awning. Even then there was good reason to suppose that his guess had been correct. The bandits were there; at any rate, somebody was there, for to his ears now came an urgent buzz of conversation. Metallic noises suggested that a vehicle was being refuelled in haste.

Had it not been for a warning shout from Ginger he might have collided with Grindler. Ginger, it transpired, caught sight of the gunman running along the fringe of the oasis, just inside the palms, from the direction of the *wadi*, as though he had waited there to intercept the crew of the Spur; but perceiving his error, he was now attempting to rectify it. He carried an automatic in each hand.

At Ginger's warning shout Biggles swerved to a tree and stopped. An instant later Grindler came into sight, taking advantage of the meagre cover available by dodging from palm to palm. The gunman saw Biggles at the same moment, and in a flash had fired two shots from the hip. But the range was long for accurate pistol work—about forty yards—and intervening palms made shooting largely a matter of luck. One bullet struck such a tree; the other whistled past the one behind which Biggles stood.

Biggles saved his ammunition. He stood still, waiting, hoping that Grindler would come on; but the gangster, while confident of his shooting, was evidently not as confident as all that, for he, too, jumped to a palm and remained still.

When two or three minutes had passed without a move being made by either side, it slowly dawned on Biggles why Grindler was apparently content with this state of affairs. His job was simply to keep him at a distance while the transport was being refuelled. If this was to be prevented, it meant that he, Biggles, would have to take the initiative. To advance in the face of Grindler's guns, while the gunman remained in cover, was clearly a project of considerable peril, for Biggles had no doubt about his opponent's ability to handle his weapons with speed and accuracy. Still, as Grindler stood between them and the spot where the transport was being refuelled, there was nothing else for it. He jumped to the next tree in the line of advance. In the instant of time occupied by the move two bullets had zipped past his face, and he knew that he was taking a desperate chance. Grindler had not shown himself; and as he held the cards there was no reason why he should.

Biggles jumped to the next palm, firing two shots as Grindler's right hand appeared, more to spoil his aim than with any real hope of hitting him. They were now not more than thirty yards apart.

Grindler sneered: 'Come on, Limey; what are you stopping for?'

How the affair would have ended had there not been a diversion is a matter for conjecture, but at this juncture there occurred an interruption which gave the situation a new twist, one that evidently surprised Grindler as much as it did Biggles. The transport's engines came to life, and at once rose to a crescendo which could only mean that the aircraft was about to take off.

It did not take Biggles long to perceive the shrewd cunning behind this move. Even though the Renkell's tanks had not been filled it was ensuring a clear start by leaving those on the oasis fully occupied with each other. Grindler was being abandoned. This was so much less weight for the machine to carry, and would result in an improved performance. A ghost of a smile flickered over Biggles' face at the thought of the gunman being left, as they say, to hold the baby. At the same time, even though he was dealing with crooks whose lack of scruples had already been proved, he was astounded at such unbelievable treachery. Not that Grindler deserved better treatment.

Biggles knew that those in the transport must have been refuelling from cans, or drums—a long process. They had not had time to completely refuel, which meant that they hoped to 'top-up' somewhere else. There was good reason to suppose that this would be Tripoli, where the airport manager would oblige them. Biggles could see the machine through the trees, heading north-west, a course that tended to confirm this theory. He heard the Spur's engine rev up, and fully expected Ginger to take off in case he should be attacked; but when it became clear that those in the transport had no such intention the Spur's engine dropped back to its low mutter.

All this had taken place much faster than it can be told, and Grindler had not been idle. When the truth—and it must have been a paralysing truth—struck him, that he was being deserted, his feelings in the matter found expression in a yell of fury. Spitting obscene vituperation he raced to the edge of the palms, and as the transport's tail lifted, blazed away at it with both guns. His chances of hitting it were, of course, remote, and he must have known it. He probably fired in sheer blind rage. Anyway, the transport gave no indication that it had been hit, and proceeded on its way.

Biggles was not so much concerned with Grindler as with the transport, because while the aircraft could continue operating without the gangster, the gangster could not go on without the aircraft. Grindler could wait, a prisoner on the oasis. All Biggles wanted was to get in the Spur in order to go on after the transport. He started backing away, but Grindler opened up such a fusillade that he was compelled to take cover in a hurry. He could not remember precisely how many shots the gunman had fired, but it struck him that the magazines of both pistols must be nearly empty. In order to find out if this were so he tried a bluff.

'You can drop those guns, Grindler, they're empty!' he shouted, at the same time emerging from cover.

'Who says they are?' snarled Grindler, also advancing.

Biggles knew he was taking a big chance, but he kept on. 'So your pal Gontermann has let you down again,' he scoffed.

Grindler choked; Biggles had never see a man's face so distorted with fury. 'That dirty, double-crossing Nazi rat,' stormed the gangster. 'I came over here to get that squealer, but he made a sucker outa me by offering to let me muscle in on this airplane racket.'

'I don't see that you've anything to complain about,' returned Biggles evenly. 'You left the Wolf to shift for itself.'

'That was Gontermann did that,' growled Grindler.

'I wonder Herr Renkell didn't stand by you,' resumed Biggles. 'He's got a clean record.'

Grindler jerked. 'That sap! He wasn't with us.'

'Not with you?'

'You bet he wasn't. We left him in that weed swamp.'

Biggles was genuinely shocked, and he looked it. 'Spare my days! You *are* a bright lot,' he sneered. 'Are you coming quietly?'

'Who said I was coming any place?' snarled Grindler.

'Please yourself,' returned Biggles. 'But make up your mind because I'm leaving. Stay here if you'd rather have it that way. You can't leave the oasis—you know that.'

'Is that so?' replied Grindler with ominous calm. 'I guess you're right, at that. Now let me tell you something, wise guy. I've got one slug left, and if I'm staying I reckon that should be enough to see that you stay, too.'

Before Biggles had fully grasped the threat that lay in the words, Grindler had spun round, and twisting like a snipe was racing towards the Spur.

Biggles fired, and missed. Before he could fire again Grindler had disappeared behind some palms. 'Look out, Ginger!' he shouted, as he set off in pursuit, aware that if the gunmen did succeed in reaching the Spur one shot in a vital place might well immobilise it—a bullet through one of the tyres would do it, for instance.

Dodging and ducking among the trees Grindler sped on. He topped a rise, and before Biggles could fire, leapt into a sort of small dell-hole beyond. Suddenly he screamed clutching at a tree; but his hand slipped, and his impetus carried him on.

The scream was cut off short by an explosion of such violence that Biggles was hurled to the ground by blast, momentarily stunned. Smoke swirled. Sand, pebbles, and pieces of palm frond pattered down. Still half dazed Biggles picked himself up and staggered to the stump of a shattered palm to get a grip on himself; then, breathing heavily, he walked on to the scene of the explosion. Just as he reached it a piece of paper came floating down. Automatically he reached for it and picked it up. On it, under a bold heading, a single line had been written in three languages—English, French, and Arabic: 'WARNING. *Beware of land mines in hollow*,' it read. It was signed '*Sergeant Mahmud, King's African Rifles*.'

Biggles climbed to the rim of the crater and looked down. Except for a few shreds of clothing, and some suggestive red stains, there was no sign of Grindler. He went on towards the Spur with some anxiety, fearing that it might have been damaged, although he hoped that an intervening dune would have saved it from the blast. It had. Ginger, looking pale and shaken, was standing in his seat.

'What in heaven's name was that?' he gasped.

'It was Grindler, falling into a nest of mines,' answered Biggles slowly. 'Sergeant Mahmud dumped them in that hollow. I suppose he had to put them somewhere, and in the ordinary way that place was as good as any. He put up a warning notice, but Grindler was in too much of a hurry to stop to read it. He fell into the dump and got the full benefit. What's left of him isn't worth picking up. He probably helped to plant the mines in the first place, so it's a nice example of poetic justice. Anyway, I'm not shedding any tears for that thug. Is the machine all right?'

'I think so,' answered Ginger. 'It danced a bit from concussion, but I fancy the worst of the blast went over us.'

'Thank God for that,' said Biggles fervently. 'We'll push on after Gontermann. The transport has taken in some petrol, but not much, I think. We barged in a bit too early for them. I should say it's making for Tripoli to top up before striking across Algeria and Morocco on the way to the States. Let's go. We haven't a lot of daylight left.'

'Personally, I haven't much of anything left,' averred Ginger. 'This show is just one place after another. Where is it going to end?'

'It will end,' answered Biggles deliberately, 'where the transport hits the carpet.*'

Looking travel-stained and weary he climbed into the cockpit, and in another minute the Spur was in the air again, heading north-west on the trail of the transport.

*Slang: hits the ground.

Chapter 18
The Last Lap

Biggles knew that by cutting in on the transport while it was refuelling he had decreased its lead by some minutes. In the case of a slow-moving vehicle, minutes, translated into terms of distance, may not amount to much; but with aircraft, able to cover the ground at seven or eight miles a minute, even seconds count. Against this advantage he had to offset the handicap that the transport had taken in an unknown quantity of fuel, so that if the chase became a test of endurance the transport would in the end outrun the Spur. He did not think it would come to that, unless Gontermann had another secret landing-ground; if he had, it seemed probable that he would now make for it, leaving the Spur with the hopeless task of finding it. Biggles did not consider this possibility seriously, because he felt that had the bandits possessed a secret refuelling station near the North African coast they would never have used a public airport like Castel Benito, at Tripoli.

As the Spur roared on, with the shadows of the dunes beginning to lengthen towards the east, Biggles perceived that the hunt was fast becoming a matter of geography. The transport was, in a manner of speaking, an outlaw, and laboured under the usual disadvantages of that condition, particularly now that it was on the run. It could only go into hiding, and obtain supplies, where friends were prepared to take the risk of accommodating it. Ruling out secret hiding-places, it was practically certain that Castel Benito aerodrome, where petrol was available and where the manager was in the swim, would be the next port of call. From there Gontermann might head north for Germany, where he would certainly have friends among the ex-Nazis prepared to offer him sanctuary. He might have to dispose of the aircraft, but he would get away with the loot. Or he might carry on due west for America, as von Zoyton had declared. America would probably suit him very well, reflected Biggles, particularly as he had now got rid of such a dangerous companion as Grindler, who was wanted by the Federal Police. But could he get there in one hop? Tripoli was still a long way from the Atlantic. The Renkell would have to have a tremendous range to take the northern Sahara in its stride, and then cross the ocean. Biggles had not forgotten that the machine had already crossed the Atlantic, but then its starting-point was unknown.

It all came to this. If the transport was able to jump from Tripoli to America, unless the Spur could catch it at Tripoli it would probably get away, because the Spur, even with full tanks, had nothing like that range; and its tanks, far from being full, were nearly empty. If the Spur had to stop to refuel at Tripoli, the transport would obtain such a lead that it would be hopeless to try to overtake it; and if the Spur went on without refuelling it would have to run the risk of running out of petrol somewhere over the desert. The immediate future, therefore, was very much in the air—literally.

Reluctantly the sand gave way to shrubs and rocky hills, while the valleys filled with verdant almond trees and silvery-grey olives. The aerodrome came into view, and Ginger surveyed the tarmac swiftly, eagerly, shielding his eyes with his hands to see the better, for they were flying almost into the orb of the setting sun, and the glare was dazzling. When he saw the unmistakable outline of the transport his satisfaction found outlet in a whoop of exultation.

'She's there!' he cried. 'We've caught her refuelling again.'

'There's another machine in the shadow of the hangar,' remarked Biggles. 'By Jupiter! It's the Swan. Preuss must be there. That's it! Now we know the meaning of the R/T signal the B.B.C. picked up. It *was* Gontermann getting into touch with Preuss, asking him to come here for some reason or other. Maybe Gontermann has an idea of dropping the transport and slipping into Germany in the Swan.'

The Spur roared on, nose down, and the aerodrome seemed to float on invisible rollers towards it; but before Biggles glided in over the boundary fence, engine idling, feverish activity was apparent round the stationary machines, although it was hard to make out just what was happening. It was obvious, however, that the arrival of the Spur had caused a commotion. A man in mechanic's overalls jumped off the transport's centre-section. Gontermann, bag in hand, dashed out of the restaurant, and started running towards the Swan; then he appeared to change his mind and made for the transport, behind which a swirl of dust revealed that its engines had been started.

At this juncture it would have been a comparatively simple matter for Biggles to shoot the transport up, but there were reasons why he hesitated to do so. The men in it were not convicted criminals, for they had not yet been tried in a court of law. Castel Benito was not the sanseviera; it was a public aerodrome; there would be spectators, witnesses who would say that the attack on the grounded machine was made without provocation—for so it would appear—and in such circumstances, if he killed the men he would be accounted little better than a murderer. Such an incident might cause a political crisis. Again, even if the men were not killed, the authorities might make a fuss over the deliberate destruction of an aircraft which, with some justification they could claim as their property. And finally, should the Renkell catch fire, the British Government might be embarrassed by the irreplacable loss of the rajah's jewels. Had the Renkell taken off and attacked the Spur the position would be altogether different. In short, while Biggles was prepared to use his guns to prevent the escape of men whom he knew were criminals and murderers, although it might not be easy to prove this, he decided first to try other methods.

The transport had swung round to face the open aerodrome, and was moving forward, slowly as yet, but with the obvious intention of taking off. To prevent this Biggles landed across its nose—or rather, it would be more correct to say that he attempted to do so. His wheels were already on the ground, so it seemed a simple matter to taxi on and block the transport's chosen runway. And no doubt it would have been, had it not been for the intervention of the Swan, which now took a hand.

Concerned primarily with the transport, after making a mental note that he could catch up with the Swan if it attempted to get away, Biggles had forgotten

211

all about it. But the yellow plane now appeared on the scene, playing the Spur's own game. That was Biggles's first impression; but he soon saw that the pilot intended more than that; for the Swan, instead of slowing down as it cut across his bows, suddenly swung round on one wheel to which the brake had been applied, and charged straight at him.

It was a clever, unexpected move, and not so dangerous to life as it might appear. The Swan had only to collide with one of the Spur's wings and the British aircraft would be grounded for an indefinite period. The collision could afterwards be described as an accident. In the meantime the transport would get clear away.

All this flashed through Biggles's mind as he took the only course open to him if collision was to be avoided. He knew that if he swerved to left or right the Swan had only to do the same to achieve its object of ramming him. So he flicked the throttle wide open, and as the Spur gathered flying speed he snatched it off the ground. It was a desperate expedient, for had his wheels failed to clear the Swan the result would have been utter and complete disaster; as it was, they missed the obstruction by a margin so narrow that the corners of Biggles's mouth were drawn down in a wave of cold anger, which was aggravated by the fact that the transport, quick to take advantage of his preoccupation, had succeeded in getting off.

As soon as he was clear, regardless of any subsequent inquiry, Biggles whirled the Spur round, and dropping his nose, slashed the Swan with a burst of fire. The pilot, presumably Preuss, might well have crashed the Spur, and that was more than Biggles was prepared to accept without retaliation. Preuss may have expected some such move, for he had stopped the Swan, jumped out, and was sprinting for the aerodrome buildings. As it happened, these were in line with Biggles's attack. For a few seconds he ran on, with bullets tearing up the sand around him; then he crashed headlong, and after rolling over and over like a shot rabbit, lay still.

'That should stop *him* laughing in church,' muttered Ginger.

'He asked for it,' grated Biggles. 'The airport manager will probably say we murdered him; which means we've burnt our boats; we've got to get the others with the swag on them, or we may find ourselves in the custard up to the neck.' Coming round in a climbing turn as he spoke, he made out the transport heading westward, having got a start of about three miles. 'We've got just one hour in which to catch them,' he remarked.

'Why an hour?' asked Ginger.

'Because, in the first place, I've got only an hour's petrol left; and secondly, in one hour from now it will be dark,' answered Biggles. 'Apart from petrol, they could give us the slip in the dark—always bearing in mind that the transport must have a lot more juice in its tanks that we have.' Biggles settled down to the chase.

In point of fact, Ginger knew that the fate of the transport would be decided in less than an hour. It would be settled in five minutes. If, in that time, they had closed the gap to any appreciable extent, they would overtake the fugitives within the hour. If the gap was not closed, it would prove that the speed of the Renkell was at least equal to their own, in which case it would certainly get away. For this reason it was with no small anxiety that he kept his eyes on the enemy aircraft.

When five or six minutes had elapsed he drew a deep breath. 'We've got 'em,' he declared, a note of triumph in his voice.

Biggles did not answer.

The Spur was on even keel at a thousand feet. The Renkell was higher, nearer two thousand, and seeing that it was being overtaken it had dropped its nose slightly. This gave it an increase of speed that enabled it to forge ahead again. But Biggles was not perturbed. Both machines were now at the same height, so the advantage gained by the transport was only temporary. The manœuvre could not be repeated successfully. Gradually the gap closed. The transport sacrificed a little more height for speed, but Biggles merely did the same, so in the end the German gained nothing by the move. All it really did was reveal its inferiority.

When twenty minutes had elapsed the distance between the two machines was less than a mile. Both were at the same height, flying directly into the sun, which now appeared to rest on the western horizon like an enormous crimson ball, casting a lurid glow across the arid waste.

Ginger looked down with some apprehension, for he knew they were running across the northern fringe of the Sahara desert, which varies a good deal in its formation. The area below appeared to have been swept clean, except for innumerable little stones which gleamed as though they had been highly polished—as, indeed, they had been, by wind and sun. The horizon was a hard, unbroken line. It was no place to run out of petrol, and Ginger began to wonder what would happen when their tanks petered out, as they would in the near future. Biggles made no move to turn back.

Over this scene, naked and helpless in its desolation, the two machines roared on, the distance between them closing slowly. Ahead, Ginger was relieved to see, the horizon was at last broken by low hills, and an occasional group of palms; but the sun had nearly run its course, and it was impossible to make out precisely what lay in front of them.

Only a quarter of a mile of heat-distorted air divided the two machines; and still the distance closed. Biggles sat quite still. His face was expressionless. Never, not for an instant, did his eyes leave his quarry.

Ginger moistened his lips, thankful that he was not in the Renkell. There was something so implacable, so relentless, about Biggles, when he was in his present mood. He knew that whatever happened he would not turn back. He would go on to the end, even if their petrol ran out and left them stranded in the heart of the Sahara.

His soliloquy was interrupted by the behaviour of the Renkell. It turned suddenly on its port wing-tip and headed south; and looking for the reason for this unexpected move Ginger saw a belt of mist hanging over a long valley, down the centre of which ran an area of swamp, or salt marsh. The mist was not coming from anywhere; it was forming in the air, now that the sun was setting, due to the difference of temperature between the sun-soaked sand and the water-cooled marsh. With a pang of alarm he realised that should the transport reach the miasma it would disappear from sight, and by changing course, lose them. Then he caught his breath with relief, for Biggles had also turned, and by cutting across the angle, brought the transport within striking distance.

After that the end came quickly. Slowly, with calculated deliberation, Biggles took the objective machine in his sights. His thumb slid over the firing button. Tracer flashed across the gap. Instantly, the transport, seeing that it could not escape, whirled round and came back at them, flecks of flame spurting from its guns, revealing for the first time the type of armament it carried. Biggles pressed his left foot gently on the rudder-bar and the transport's tracer streamed past his right wing-tip. The Renkell hurtled past. The Spur was already turning, and in a split second Biggles was on the transport's tail. Again his tracer flashed, the shots converging on the target. The Renkell zoomed wildly, and turned vertically at the top of its climb; but it made no difference; the Spur was still behind it, firing short, vicious bursts.

Then a strange thing happened. The escape hatch of the transport opened and a man's figure dropped earthward. An instant later a parachute mushroomed.

'Gontermann. He can't take it,' said Biggles, and went on after the transport, which was now barely under control. It went into a dive that became steeper and steeper, and Ginger could hear the screams of its airscrews above the roar of their own. He bit his lip, knowing what was going to happen. He had seen it happen before. Biggles was no longer firing.

The dive of the stricken machine steepened until it was going down vertically. Ginger flinched when the crash came. With the languid deliberation of a slow-motion screen picture the aircraft seemed to disintegrate, and spread itself over the desert. He knew that no one inside the machine could have survived such a fearful impact.

Biggles circled once or twice, losing height, and then, flying a few feet above the sand, went on after Gontermann who, still carrying his bag, was running towards the swamp.

'To the last, all he thought about was himself,' said Biggles grimly. 'He hadn't the guts to see it through. What a skunk the fellow must be.'

He landed the Spur between the swamp and the running man, jumped down, and after walking a few paces, took out his pistol and waited.

Gontermann also stopped, snatching a glance at the desert behind him.

'Go that way if you like,' sneered Biggles.'Your carcass should poison the vultures, when they find you.'

Gontermann hesitated.

'Come on—come on; you've got a gun,' invited Biggles. 'Use it or drop it. I don't care which.'

Gontermann advanced a few paces. 'Listen, Bigglesworth,' he called in a high-pitched voice. 'What I've got in this bag will make us the two richest men on earth. I'm willing to split two ways. All I ask is, you give me a lift—'

'Shut up,' snapped Biggles. 'You make me sick. Drop that bag and get your hands up.'

Gontermann stood the bag on the desert sand. All the arrogance had gone out of him. 'Don't shoot,' he pleaded.

'Put your hands up and keep walking,' said Biggles coldly.

The Nazi walked forward, slowly, nervously. 'All

right. I'll come quietly,' he said. 'I know when I'm beaten.'

'Okay.' Biggles returned the pistol to his pocket, or had started to do so, when Gontermann moved with the speed of light. His hand flashed to his side and came up holding a heavy calibre Mauser*.

Biggles's gun spat, and the Nazi seemed to stiffen. Yet he managed to get his pistol up and fire. But Biggles had side-stepped. Again his gun cracked. Again Gontermann stiffened convulsively. The muzzle of the Mauser sagged; it exploded into the ground, making the sand spurt; then the weapon dropped with a gentle thud. The man who had held it sank to his knees, and then slid forward, like a swimmer in smooth water.

Biggles stood still for a moment, watching, before walking forward to look at the fallen man.

'Pity,' he said quietly to Ginger, who now came running up. 'I would rather have taken him alive—but perhaps it's better this way. I daren't take a chance with him in a place like this. He was as crooked as a dog's hind leg; even at the finish he tried to spring one on me. Well, it's spared the country the expense of a trial, and saved the hangman a job. Let's see what's happened over here.' He walked on to the crash. Now that Gontermann was dead his anger seemed to have burnt itself out like a wisp of paper.

As they expected, there was only one man in the wreck—Baumer. He was dead.

'I still don't understand why they left Renkell in the sanseviera,' said Biggles. 'He may still be alive. When

*German automatic pistol.

218

we go back to Khartoum to see how Bertie's getting on we'll see if we can find him.'

'What I should like to know,' said Ginger, 'is how we're going to get out of this devil's dustbin with empty tanks.'

'Not quite empty,' reminded Biggles. 'We've still a drop in hand, and I reckon we're not many miles south of the French Air Force landing-ground at Touggourt. There's another one, Ouargla, a little to the south. As a matter of fact, there are quite a bunch of desert aerodromes in front of us—Colomb Bechar, Beni Abbes . . . Hallo! What's this coming?' He broke off, gazing into the darkening eastern sky, whence came the drone of an aircraft.

'Mosquito,' said Ginger. 'That'll be Algy. He must have had a word with the manager bloke at Castel Benito, and ascertained the course we took. He can't miss seeing us on this blistering billiard table.'

The Mosquito came on, roaring at full throttle a few hundred feet above the sand.

'Poor old Algy,' said Biggles, smiling. 'He still hopes to be in at the finish. Ah-ha! He's seen us.'

The Mosquito had altered course and was now standing directly towards them. The bellow of its engines died away; its wheels came down, and very soon it was on the sand, taxi-ing towards the Spur. Algy leapt out.

'What's happened?' he asked quickly.

'It's all over,' answered Biggles. 'Baumer stuck to his ship and went into the deck fast enough to break every bone in his body. Gontermann baled out. He tried to plug me, so I had to let him have it. I aimed at his arm, but hit him in the chest. My shooting must be getting shaky.'

'After the flying you've done today I'm not surprised at that,' asserted Algy. 'What are we going to do?'

Biggles thought for a moment. 'We shall have to leave things here as they are. I don't see what else we can do—unless you feel like turning your kite into a hearse. We'll make for Algiers—that's the nearest airport—and send a cable to Raymond from there. No doubt he'll ask the French authorities to take care of this mess. In the morning I'll push on to London in the Mosquito, taking Gontermann's collection of sparklers with me. They should cure Raymond's headache. You two can drift back to Khartoum in the Spur, in your own time, to see how Bertie's getting on. We'd better be moving, before it's quite dark.'

He walked over to Gontermann's bag, and opening it, gazed for a moment at its scintillating contents. 'While this sort of rubbish clutters up civilisation I suppose there will always be crooks,' he remarked. Then a smile spread slowly over his face. 'Still, ten per cent of that little lot should keep us in cigarettes for a day or two.' He closed the bag, stood up, and passed his hand wearily over his face. 'Strewth! I'm tired. Let's get along.'

The story of a chase should end with the death or capture of the quarry, but in this case one or two points remain to be cleared up.

By noon of the day following the final affair in the desert Biggles was at Scotland Yard. As a matter of detail he had slept at Gibraltar, from where he had been able to send a signal through service channels to

Air Commodore Raymond, who was at Croydon Airport to meet him. At the Yard, an inventory was made of the contents of Gontermann's bag, which, besides the rajah's regalia, included the best of the pearls of the Persian Gulf affair, and the South African diamonds.

'Ten per cent, sir, I think you said?' murmured Biggles blandly.

The Air Commodore looked up with a twinkle in his eye. 'I doubt if any policeman earned so much in so short a time. You'd better stay in the Force and make your fortune.'

'It has to be shared four ways, don't forget,' reminded Biggles. 'Still, I'll think about your suggestion,' he added.

After writing a detailed report on the whole operation, he had a bath, changed, and later dined with the Commissioner of Police, and his assistant, Air Commodore Raymond. That night he had his first unbroken sleep for some time.

In the morning he started back for Khartoum to see how Bertie was faring. He found him out of danger, although the doctor predicted that the injured leg might shorten a trifle, so that he would probably limp for the rest of his life.

'I asked him to cut a piece off the other, to get 'em the same length again—if you see what I mean?' complained Bertie. 'But the silly ass wouldn't do it. Said he might slice off too much, and then I should go into a permanent bank the other way—or some such rot.'

Algy and Ginger had flown on to the sanseviera. They came back some time after Biggles's arrival, bringing with them Herr Renkell, whom they had spotted wandering in the swamp. The aircraft designer declared that far from having any hand in the disappearance of his prototypes, he had been abducted by the bandits and forced to act as mechanic on his own machines, the idea being, presumably, that, as the designer, he was the only man who thoroughly understood them. Biggles believed him. Indeed, his appearance did much to confirm his story, for he looked thin and ill. He declared, and Algy verified, that the whole area occupied by the secret landing-ground had been burnt out, as well as the equipment, oil, and petrol.

Biggles inquired after von Zoyton, but being told that he was still on the danger list, and not allowed visitors, he did not see him. This had a curious sequel. Weeks later, when Biggles and his comrades were back in London, they learned that not only had von Zoyton recovered from his injuries, but had taken advantage of a *haboob*—one of the local violent sand-storms—to make his escape from hospital. The Egyptian police were looking for him, but so far had been unsuccessful.

'I'm not altogether sorry,' said Biggles, when he heard this news. 'He wasn't a bad chap at heart. Probably it all came from getting mixed up with the wrong crowd when he was a kid. His mother should have warned him.'